Misfortune's Wake

Also by Joe Kilgore

Insomniac: Short Stories for Long Nights

The Brig Ellis Tales

Fool's Errand

Cast Them Dead

and coming soon...

Carrion Moon

Misfortune's Wake

JOE KILGORE

Encircle Publications
Farmington, Maine, U.S.A.

Cover design by Christopher Wait
Cover photographs © Getty Images

Published by:

Encircle Publications
PO Box 187
Farmington, ME 04938

info@encirclepub.com
http://encirclepub.com

To Deirdre, Chris, Cynthia, and Eddie
for past, present, and future

"There are no secrets that time does not reveal."
—Jean Racine

Chapter 1

At Punto Olvidado Bay the cove beckons, but beneath glistening turquoise waters, silent soldiers stand vigil. Ageless rocks lie in wait, their jagged dorsals capable of ripping hulls asunder should impatient sailors attempt a landing without benefit of caution or experience. That's what Russell had been told by the man who rowed him through the boulders fronting the beach. A bit like life, the young American thought. The promise of peace and respite transforms into chaos and woe if not given the respect it deserves. There is a price to be paid for beauty and solace, he reflected, often a very high price.

Russell rolled up his pant legs, used his laces to tie his shoes together, then slung them over his shoulder as he swung himself over the side of the boat and into the shallow water. The chill was bracing as his toes dug into the sand giving him purchase to stride past the lethargic waves gently teasing the beach. Battered valise in one hand, he used the other to wave farewell to the boatman.

Per his instructions, he walked up the hill to the side of the road. A vehicle was to arrive at the top of the hour to complete the last leg of his journey. The agreed-upon time came and went, but Russell didn't. He waited patiently, assuming punctuality wasn't as important here as it was where he came from. His wait and his view allowed him to see the dingy return to the ship, where it was hoisted aboard before the vessel headed back to the open sea. Russell wondered for a moment whether his past might be leaving with it. Yet deep down, he sensed that the past continually lingers, unobtrusively if one is lucky, but always on call in an unexpected shadow or a night without something to initiate sleep.

Eventually, a lorry approached. It was old and battered, not unlike the man who drove it. The driver saw the sandy-haired, blue-eyed foreigner sitting on his valise by the side of the road. There were sweat rings under his arms and his sleeves were rolled up to his biceps. Surely this was the man he was sent to retrieve. A nod of the driver's head and a smile revealing discolored teeth prompted Russell to inquire if this was the ride he'd been waiting for.

"Retiro de Santos?"

"Sí, señor."

Moments later Russell was in the passenger seat with his arm resting on the window sill. The wind whipping by as they drove helped modify the oily smell of the interior and its occupant behind the wheel. Even sitting down, the lanky American dwarfed the driver. He seemed a nice old man, Russell thought. Though English was far from the fellow's understanding, and the American's Spanish was only minimal, they passed the trip occasionally smiling at one another and staring out the cracked, dirty windshield at the glory of the mountain and the sea. The old man had seen both infinitely more times than he could count. For Russell, it was new and ablaze with sun-filled hope.

On the far side of the mountain, they came down through heavy jungle as their path became more arduous over a road jutted by rain and time. Going was slow. Russell wondered how long it would take to reach town, but he knew that asking was futile. The old man would not understand him and he'd probably botch the question anyway. So they traveled at the pace the weathered trail dictated and the American contented himself with the fact that at least they were moving forward.

Eventually, the dirt and gravel flattened into something resembling a paved road, with its share of requisite potholes. Soon a winding stretch was negotiated, then a hill was climbed, and when the lorry topped it, Russell got his first look at Retiro de Santos.

Well, certainly not grand, he thought. Quaint. That's the word for it, he decided. Narrow streets of brick and cobblestone. Bright colors of yellow, pink, and blue, adorned the walls of shops, houses, and cafés. Thatched roofs here and there. The jungle had been cut away to make room for the degree of civilization that initially encroached upon it, but now it looked as if the lush green palm trees, ferns, moss, and cacti were starting to reclaim their territory. Glass was not prominent. Windows were framed by shutters that could be opened, closed, and locked via rope ties. Ornamental iron gates fronted a few buildings.

There were not many people on the street. It was the time of day when heat encouraged most to stay indoors. Russell was hesitant to give the driver a specific location. He assumed the man had his instructions. A few twists and turns into the heart of town confirmed Russell's assumption. The lorry came to a halt just outside a two-story adobe structure whose blandness silently suggested a municipal building of some sort. The old man smiled, nodded his head, and pointed toward the front door with bars across its one square window.

"*Gracias*," Russell said, returning a smile and wondering if he should offer a gratuity for the ride. Would the fellow appreciate it or find it discourteous? Not wanting to chance the latter, he opened his door, stepped out, and paused to see if the driver was waiting for a tip. But the old man simply smiled again as he put the vehicle in gear, nodded, then drove slowly away. As he waved goodbye, Russell hoped he had made the right decision. Not only the one regarding the driver, but also his decision to come to this place. He wasn't certain it was the right thing to do. These days he wasn't certain about a lot of things.

Chapter 2

The dried and broken sticks that made up the kindling were wrapped in flower sacks that had been sown together and draped across the back of the burro. She walked beside the little animal, guiding him with the rope that ringed his neck. It had been decided that she was old enough now to take the wood into town. Not decided by her of course, but by her father who made all decisions regarding Elena and his other children. At sixteen, she was tall for her age, lithe of limb, and striking. Her dark brows were set over aqua eyes, a thin nose, and full lips. She had begun to turn many heads in the village.

The bundles born by the donkey would bring only a few meager pesos, but each one was a godsend for her family. They would help put whatever food that could not be grown, caught, or killed, on their table. The little beast seemed unfazed by the weight. Pepito, as she called him, was used to working hard. As he walked, she would run her hand across the top of his head and between his ears. He would seldom respond, but she sensed that he liked it.

Elena was the oldest of her siblings. She had two brothers and a sister. All worked as if they were no longer children. Perhaps they never had been. The boys toiled with her father in the fields, or in the tiny boat when he fished for their evening meal. Her sister, the youngest of the brood, would help their mother shell peas and shuck corn. Everyone had responsibilities, poverty being an equal opportunity taskmaster.

As Elena walked, she daydreamed. Looking up at the sky, the billowing clouds became satin and brocade dresses she had seen in discarded magazines by the side of the road. The wind blowing the palm fronds ignited a memory of shimmering dancers she had watched on the television in the window of Marquez's store. There was a world beyond this one, she silently told herself. A world where girls didn't have to live their lives in houses with dirt floors and grass roofs. Proof came in the form of tourists clad in crop tops, shorts, and sandals, their hair blowing in the wind as they drove too fast down forest trails in those pink and white open-topped cars from the hotel. Some of the girls she had known growing up worked there now, cleaning rooms, changing sheets, wiping toilets she and her family did not have. Perhaps she could do this one day. It seemed a goal that might be within reach, perhaps, if her father changed his mind. He almost never did, but one could wish. It made the days endurable.

Father Alonso was tending his small garden behind the church when he saw Elena and Pepito coming down the path that would take them into the heart of town. The short priest with hair the color of charcoal and eyes to match, wiped his brow with a handkerchief, put down his hoe, and walked over to greet her.

"*Buenos días*, Elena. How are you this morning?" The priest would insert English into conversations with those of his flock who could understand him. He knew some degree of English would be helpful, especially to the young ones.

"*Estoy bien*, Padre. I am well. ¿*Y tú*?"

"A little hot. A little tired. It seems one my age always is."

"You are not so old, Father Alonso."

"Thirty-five is three and one-half decades, little one. Is that not old?"

"*Sí*. Is much older than me. But not too old."

"You are kind. And I see Pepito is working this day?"

"We go to town to sell the… the… *astillas*."

"The kindling."

"*Sí*. I mean, yes. The kindling."

"And your family?"

"They are well."

"You will give my regards to your father when you return?"

"I will," she responded. Though the priest could tell it was with some reluctance.

"Is he still considering what you shared with me?"

"I think so, Father. He knows I don't want to do it. But he says everyone must help the family."

"Life is difficult… *defícil*… for all, Elena."

"I know, Father. But I could do something else. I could work at the hotel."

"Sadly, the hotel cannot employ everyone."

"But it is wrong, Father. You know such a thing is wrong."

"I know, my child. I will speak to him again. But he is stubborn… *obstinado*. And in your family, there are many mouths to feed."

"But you will try, Father?"

"I will. I will try again to reason with him."

"Thank you, Father."

"You are a good soul, Elena. You will remain a good soul whatever happens."

Father Alonso put two fingers to his lips, then pressed them against her forehead, She did her best to smile as she and Pepito turned and continued on their way.

Chapter 3

Russell opened the door and stepped inside. He saw a single desk in the middle of a virtually empty room—empty save for the rack of rifles and shotguns attached to one wall. Behind the desk, a fat man in a wrinkled uniform sat with his attention focused on the newspaper he was holding. He made no effort to put the paper down or address him. So Russell approached and saw a name tag on the man's shirt. It read: Officer Garza.

"Hello, Officer Garza. My name is Stephen Russell. Do you speak English?"

"*Poco*," came the reply.

"I'm new here, but I was told I'd need to check in with the local authorities."

"Resident? Or *tourista*?"

"Uh, resident. I'm going to be living here."

Finally, putting the paper down, Garza said, "You wait."

Then rising, not without difficulty due to his excessive bulk, he proceeded to amble across the room to a doorway where he stopped, knocked, and waited until he heard "*Entrar*," then entered and closed the door behind him.

As Russell lingered, he reminded himself that he'd been told to expect a slower pace in Retiro de Santos. His trek from the beach and this temporary—he hoped—pause confirmed that he had received insightful advice. In a little over a minute, which seemed infinitely longer, the portly man stepped out and waved Russell over.

"*El Comandante Delgado te verá ahora.*"

Russell was attempting to translate when he heard a voice on the other side of the door.

"He said that I will see you now. Please come in."

As Russell entered, Garza left and closed the door behind him. An altogether different individual was behind the desk. As he stood and extended his hand, Russell noted he was the polar opposite of the rumpled fellow who initially greeted him. This man stood tall, over six feet. His uniform was starched. A sidearm was at his trim waist. His black hair was cut neatly and combed straight back. A thin mustache rode rakishly over his mouth.

"I am Comandante Delgado of the police constabulary. My Sergeant indicated you are a new resident of Retiro de Santos?"

"Well, I plan to be, yes. Actually, I've just arrived. My name is Stephen Russell."

"Please, Mr. Russell, have a seat."

As Russell slipped into one of the two straight-back chairs in front of the comandante's desk, he took quick stock of the surroundings. Neat. Orderly. Papers in stacks, not strewn about the desk. The walls were blank, however. No family pictures. No calendars. No framed degrees, training certifications, or any of the sorts of things one might expect to find in someone's office.

"You speak English very well, Comandante."

"And that surprises you?"

"No. Not really. It's just that my Spanish is pretty pedestrian, and I'm happy to find someone in authority who is easy to converse with."

"Well, since English it seems is the international language, and since the British and Americans seem to be in no hurry to learn other tongues, we do our part."

"Yes, well your part is certainly appreciated by me. While I hope to become a lot more fluent while I'm here, I'm afraid my mastery of your language will never match yours of mine."

"Thank you for that compliment. Even in—what I've heard described by some of your compatriots—as a "backwater" such as this, we are not averse to flattery. Assuming it is sincere."

"I assure you it is. And as for being a backwater, well that's certainly not how I feel. I've been struck by the natural beauty ever since I arrived."

"And when was that, Mr. Russell?"

"Let me see," he said, looking at his watch. "About two hours ago."

"Ah, I see. I admire a man who can make... how do you say it... snap decisions."

"First impressions are frequently the correct ones."

"Frequently. Perhaps. Though not always, yes? Tell me, why have you come to Retiro de Santos? And what can I do for you?"

"I'm with the WCO... the World Conservation Organization. I'm going to be taking Mr. Thackery's place here."

"Oh yes. Mr. Neil Thackery. I know him. Though I was not aware he was leaving."

"Yes. In about a week, I think. He needs to take me through everything first."

"And, are you also interested in *tortugas*?"

"Turtles? Yes. Sea Turtles. The big ones. I'm looking forward to learning more about them and their nesting grounds. Thackery is supposed to show me the ropes."

"The ropes?"

"Oh, that's just an expression. I mean Thackery's supposed to orient me, you know. Give me information about what's to be done and how to do it."

"This is your first posting then, with the WCO?"

"Yes. It is?

"And before that?"

"I was a teaching assistant at the college I attended."

"And your field of study was?"

"English literature. I was planning on becoming a teacher."

"Really? From teaching to *tortugas*? A rather strange progression."

"Yes, well… I… got sidetracked a bit. Decided to do something totally different for a while. Figured I could always go back to teaching if this doesn't turn out to be something I want to stick with."

"I admire your ability to choose your own profession… to do what you want to do, not what you have to do. People in other parts of the world are not so lucky."

"That's true. Not everyone has the same opportunities. I hope to make the most of mine."

"And just how can I help in that regard, Señor Russell?"

"Well, I was told to check in with the local authorities when I first arrived. So, that's what I'm doing."

"Very kind of you to be so prompt. This is a mere formality. I simply need to see your passport, make a copy of it, and record where you'll be staying in Retiro de Santos. It is both for your safety and that of the community. By knowing where you are, we are better able to help should any emergencies arise."

"I'll be staying with Thackery during this orientation period. After he leaves, I'll be living where he did. The WCO actually covers the rent. It's part of the package because the salary's so meager."

"And why would an American college graduate take a

position with a less-than-attractive salary? Especially one who planned to work in another field."

"Well, as I said, I got a bit sidetracked. Wanted to get away to someplace different. Seemed like this filled the bill. Here's my passport."

Delgado took it, thumbed through it momentarily, then flipped to the section he needed while turning to the machine behind his desk and making a copy.

When he handed it back to the American he said, "Now Señor Russell, we know where you'll be and you know where we are. So do not hesitate should you need to contact us."

"Well, I do have one immediate need?"

"And what would that be?"

"I have Thackery's address. But I'm not at all sure how to get there."

"He is not coming into town to pick you up?"

"No. I couldn't be positive of my arrival time today, so I just told him I'd come to him."

"It is only a short walk from here to the hotel. Simply turn to the right when you step outside. They have a hired car there and someone who will take you to Thackery's."

"His place is not hard to find?"

"You'll soon realize that no place is hard to find here, Señor Russell. That's part of the charm of Retiro de Santos."

Chapter 4

The sun had already begun its downward arc toward the sea when Father Alonso came upon Miguel Esperaza, Elena's father, and her two brothers. They were pulling a small wooden skiff into shore when the priest walked to the water's edge to meet them. Pablo and Esteban tugged with all their might to make sure the boat could rest beyond the soon-to-be outgoing tide. Miguel reached in and assured his basket with the day's catch of snapper and mackerel was secure. Then he lifted it to take it with him.

"*Hola*, Miguel," the priest shouted as he neared. "Fishing was good today?"

"Enough for a family's supper, Father. Perhaps enough for more if you would care to join us."

"*Gracias*, Miguel. You are most kind. But I cannot join you this evening. If I could I would be bringing something for the table."

"Can you not turn these few fish into enough to feed the masses, like you say Jesus did?"

"I am not a maker of miracles, Miguel. Just a poor country priest."

"And I, as you know, am not a believer in miracles. Once these fish are cooked, they will be enough to feed our family tonight, nothing more."

"Indeed, you are a practical man, Miguel. That is why I wanted to talk to you."

"Boys," Miguel shouted, "come take these fish and run home to your mother so she can begin preparing them. Father Alonso and I will follow."

The boys took the basket from their father and raced to the trail that would take them back to their home.

"I saw Elena today," Father Alonso began, "taking Pepito to town to sell kindling."

"Yes. She is old enough now. For that task and others."

"It is other tasks that I wanted to talk to you about, Miguel. Tasks that might not be best for someone like Elena."

"What do you know of tasks for daughters? Priests have no children."

"My flock are all my children, Miguel. Both the young and the old."

"Children of the spirit, Father. Not children of your loins. There is a difference."

"Both are children of love. In that way, they are the same."

"I have to feed my children. You do not. In that way, they are different."

"I try to feed my children with the love of God, Miguel."

"And I feed my children with real food, Father. They would not grow very big or last very long with only the love of God."

"As I said, you are a practical man, Miguel. A practical man is hard to reason with."

"That is because I deal in reality. The reality of today and tomorrow. Not fairy tales."

"I wish you were a believer, Miguel."

"I wish these five fish in my basket were fifty. Wishing does not make it so."

Father Alonso paused momentarily. While he could quote scripture verbatim, he often found it challenging to engage in debate with non-believers. They seemed to have questions and answers for everything. Many of the questions, he actually shared himself. But he never let others know it. Frequently he would simply reply that the lord works in strange ways. More often than not, it only stopped conversation. He realized another approach was needed.

"Elena tells me you have plans for her future."

"Elena talks too much. And shares family plans she should not."

"She is a good girl, Miguel. Too good for Simone's house."

"She can make more money in Simone's house in one weekend than she can doing anything else for a month."

"But what she'll have to do to earn it… it is not right… it is against God's will."

"It is the same thing she would have to do to make a husband happy, Father. She will just be making other husbands happy. And most of all, she will be helping her brothers, and mother, and…"

"You, too?"

"Yes, she will be helping me also, to help the family grow and prosper."

"But at what cost to herself, Miguel?"

"A cost she can afford. A cost she can get over. Many of Simone's girls go on to have ordinary lives once they leave her employ."

"And some do not. Some succumb to the guilt and sin."

"Sin is your department, Father. And anyway, you say you can absolve people of sins."

"I don't absolve. God absolves. But he asks that people go and sin no more."

"And if they don't. You… or you speaking for him… tell them the same thing when they come in the next time and make their confession. Why should sinners stop now if they can stop later, Father? It is the way of the world."

"But the way of the world is not always the right way."

"Right or wrong, it is the way *this* world works."

"And what about that next world, Miguel? What about everlasting life after death? What do you think will happen to you if you force your own daughter into a life of sin?"

"I worry about one world at a time, Father. I have mouths to feed now. So, I worry about this world. I will worry about some other world if and when I come to it."

"By then it may be too late."

"It is late now, Father, and I am tired, as I always am this time of day. The road forks here. I will take my leave of you."

"*Sí.* Farewell, Miguel. Perhaps we will talk again soon."

"Perhaps."

Father Alonso was about to say, "*Vaya con Dios.*" But he wasn't sure Miguel wanted God to be with him, or perhaps even vice versa. So he said nothing and took the road that led back to his church.

Chapter 5

The makeshift taxi let Russell out in front of Thackery's place. The American looked at the building halfway up the hill and hoped it was more structurally sound than it appeared. Wooden slats formed the walls. The floor and porch consisted of adjacent two-by-fours. A somewhat cantilevered roof extended beyond the railing that framed the front of the bungalow, cottage, or perhaps the word Russell found most appropriate, shack. He noticed a trail of flat sandstone rocks leading up the grade, so he decided to take it. Midway he heard a voice.

"Russell? Stephen Russell? Is that you?"

Russell spotted a ruddy fellow with red hair wearing a T-shirt, shorts, and thick horn-rimmed glasses peering down at him from the porch. "G'day. I'm Neil Thackery. Come on up. Just follow the stones."

When Russell reached the stairs leading to the front door, Thackery met him at the top. He held two bottles of beer in one hand and took the American's valise with his other.

"Let me give you a hand with that, mate. I'll just set it by the door. Thought you might like a cold one," he said, handing one of the beers to Russell.

"I would indeed. Thanks very much."

"Here's to fancy times and friendly Sheilas," Thackery intoned, as he clinked his beer against the one he'd given to his visitor.

"Don't see how I can argue with a toast like that. I didn't know you were Australian."

"Noticeable, is it?" he asked jokingly. "Well, we're all from somewhere, aren't we? Where's your particular neck of the woods, as you Yanks like to say."

"I'm from Oklahoma. Middle of the states, you know?"

"I do know. Been to America once or twice. Got to Texas once, but never Oklahoma."

"It's doesn't necessarily top the lists of tourist destinations."

"Nor does Alice Springs. That's where I'm from. Northern Territory. Guess us landlocked boys are always trying to get to the coast in one way or another, right?"

Russell immediately liked the Aussie's informal and friendly demeanor. The fact that they shared a common language, if not a common accent, helped. Thackery was easy to listen to and apparently enjoyed hearing himself talk as well. He was more than happy to fill Russell in on his wandering ways without probing too deeply into his guest's. That suited Russell, who was used to keeping a tight rein on what he revealed to others. The two bantered back and forth until they'd finished their beers. Then Thackery suggested they go inside so Russell could get a peek at the walls that would be surrounding him as a new resident of Retiro de Santos.

"It's not much, but it's priced right," Thackery quipped as they stepped into an open room that was a combined living, sleeping, and dining area. A small stove and refrigerator were behind a bar in one corner of the room; on the opposite stood two doors.

"Door on the left's the closet. The dunny's in there. Got a shower and everything. All the comforts of home. Sleeping this week, you take the bed, I'll set up a cot in that corner."

"Oh no. Let me take the cot," Russell quickly responded. "You shouldn't have to compromise your last week here."

"Good on you, mate. Nice to know they grow gentlemen on those Oklahoma prairies. Why don't you take a couple of minutes to stow your gear and wash up? I'll get us a couple more cold ones. Then we can gab a bit about what you'll be doing while you're here. No need to visit the beach until tomorrow. I was out earlier. Got the whole week to get you indoctrinated. As they say, Rome wasn't built in a day. And having met a few Italians in my time, I can understand why."

Russell opened the closet door and was in the process of swinging his bag up and onto a shelf when he realized he was now eye to eye with a coatimundi. The little fellow's pointed nose and masked eyes looked squarely into the American's face, as the coati's ringed tail curled around the valise handle.

"Jesus!" Russel exclaimed, springing backward.

"No. Not Jesus. That's Bolivar," Thackery injected. "He sort of comes with the property. Was here when I came. Will be here when I leave. Got a feeling he'll be here when you leave, too."

"Does he bite?"

"Only fruits and berries. And the occasional insect, bird, lizard, or you'll be happy to hear, snake. Think of him as your live-in security."

"Will I need to feed him?"

"Oh, he'll do nicely on his own. But don't be surprised if he occasionally wants a bite of your chicken or fish. I'd let him have it if I were you, mate."

Chapter 6

Comandante Delgado's phone rang and the number appeared on its screen. He recognized it and could have answered immediately, but not wanting to appear subservient, let it sound off two more times before picking up the receiver.

"Delgado here."

"I understand the new WCO man has arrived."

"That appears to be the case. You found out rather quickly."

"We all have our sources."

"Some apparently better than others," Delgado replied. "I was not aware Thackery was leaving, or that he was to be replaced."

"I believe the Australian went out of his way to keep a lid on his impending departure. Doesn't trust people, I suppose."

"Perhaps. Regardless, a newcomer complicates things. We may have to start over."

"What was your take on this new fellow?"

Pausing for a moment before answering, Delgado said, "In some ways, he may be easier. Younger. Not particularly experienced. He did not strike me as a zealot. Idealistic, I assume."

"You know what they say, Comandante. Not an idealist in

your twenties and you have no heart. Not a conservative in your forties and you have no brain."

"I get the feeling this is one of those who feel they can fuel their idealism by conserving. Stopping progress to preserve the past for the future."

"Convoluted as it sounds, isn't it?"

"Change is inevitable. It is, in fact, the only constant."

"Yes, we know that, but the Thackery's and the... remind me of this new man's name."

Looking down at the note he had made in his desk calendar, Delgado answered, "Russell. Stephen Russell."

"Yes. The Thackerys and the Russells of this planet have yet to see the world through our practical eyes. More's the pity."

"Getting back to Thackery," Delgado interjected. "How much do you think he will share with this Russell?"

"Hard to say. He may want to impart whatever insight he thinks he has, or he may simply want to get out as quickly and cleanly as he can."

"I have never cared for Thackery. His manner offends."

"Does bray a bit, doesn't he? Ingrained personality defect, I suspect. They're all prison stock, you know."

"Environmentalists?"

"Australians."

"I will find out what I can," Delgado offered. "Perhaps he has spoken with others about his leaving."

"And I'll look into this new fellow. Send me a copy of his passport. I might touch base with some people and arrange sort of a soirée. A combination going-away for Thackery plus a bit of a meet-and-greet for Russell. The Australian won't be able to turn down free drinks and the American will feel compelled to make nice. We might learn something from one or the other that could prove valuable."

"I will be on the guest list?"

"Comandante, it wouldn't be a party without you."

Chapter 7

Russell hadn't slept well. The cot was less than comfortable. Being tired from his trip, however, enabled him to get at least some rest. He awoke to Thackery's banging on the stove, preparing what he would later refer to as a big fry-up: eggs, chorizo, potatoes, toast, and coffee. Both men attacked it ravenously.

There were two ways to get to that section of the beach that served as a nesting ground for the sea turtles. One was to leave from the front of the cabin, go down to the road, and walk around the hillside; a half-hour jaunt. The other was to leave from the back, hike over the hill, and down to the beach; steeper going up and more precarious coming down, but shorter by a third. Thackery decided the latter would be a good test of Russell's physical condition, so up and over they went.

Coming out of the dense growth that led down to the shoreline, the American was winded but had managed to traverse the terrain without falling. Thackery was suitably impressed.

"Good show, mate. First time I took this path I wound up ass over elbows a couple of times."

"Had a few stumbles, but thankfully, managed to keep my feet."

"So, what do you think?"

"Beautiful. Just beautiful."

Russell was gazing at a stretch of white beach that ran six hundred yards from a natural fortress of rocks bordering it on one side to a sharp curve of shoreline on the other. The water that lapped up and back languidly had a milky appearance in the shallows due to the color of the sand. For a hundred feet or so, deep pockets were scattered beneath the surface making the water above them appear emerald. Then the sea floor dropped off entirely and a stretch of turquoise eventually turned lapis blue.

"It's a stunner, all right," Thackery added. "What say we check it out."

As they walked along the tide's edge, their conversation turned to those they had signed on to help. Looking out at the ocean, Russell said, "It's really amazing, isn't it? The fact that they can travel hundreds, even thousands of miles and still find their way back to nest."

"They're crafty buggers, all right… navigating the earth's magnetic field to find their way home. Bit of a built-in compass, you know. Sometimes wish we humans had one."

"You need help getting home now and then?" Russell asked.

"Depends entirely on the number of cold ones consumed. Must admit I've been known to head off in the wrong direction a time or two."

"Are there specific places along here where they lay their eggs? Do I need to be aware of those?"

"I can show you some of the spots," Thackery answered, "they're all well above the tide line. But you have to keep an eye on the entire area. Sometimes you'll find 'em one place, sometimes another. That's why the job is to look out for the entire stretch of beach."

Moving from the waterline up, Russell tried to wrap his mind around the incredible challenge nature had set up for these creatures. Once their eggs were laid, sometimes as many as a hundred or more at a time, they were subject to all sorts of hazards—animals scrounging for food, people trampling in places where they shouldn't be, litter washed up on shore, storms that sent tides well beyond their original boundaries. Then, for those eggs that were lucky enough to hatch, there was the long trek to the water's edge. Not that far if you walk on two feet and stand upright. But almost forever if you're the size of the last knuckle on a little finger. Surely that's why only one or two hatchlings out of literally thousands ever make it to adulthood, Russell thought. Survival of the fittest can be incredibly cruel, and not just in the animal kingdom.

"Let's go over by the rocks," Thackery said. "Someone there I want you to get acquainted with."

As they walked toward the boulders running from the base of the hill to the water, Russell assumed Thackery knew of some exotic animal nearby, like the coatimundi, Bolivar, who shared their quarters. Russell prepared himself to be appropriately surprised, but the closer he got to the rock formation, he realized that he hadn't prepared himself for one of the boulders to move.

"What the…"

"Stephen, meet Minerva," Thackery said. "I assume your first leatherback."

"You assume correctly," Russell managed to answer, as the enormous turtle began to separate itself from its camouflage. "My God, how much does she weigh?"

"Clocks in at about 1,800 pounds. When she's tucked into the rocks, most people don't know she's there. Like you, a few moments ago. I've been here long enough to be able to spot her from a distance."

"Is she heading toward the water now?"

"Indeed. Going to take a dip. Maybe even have a bit of jellyfish for lunch."

"How long will she be gone?"

"Can't say. That's up to her. Likes the shallower waters 'cause they're warmer. But once she decides to dive, she could stay under for hours. Haven't really been able to document a specific schedule. She pretty much comes and goes as she pleases. But of course, that's what we're here for. To make sure she and others can continue to do that."

"Are people around here aware of her?"

"If so," Thackery responded, "it's not because of me. I keep things quiet as I can. At the moment, no one's supposed to be on this beach without permission. But word gets around that this is a sea turtle habitat, and it's impossible to keep tourists or curious locals away all the time. The natural barriers help. Mostly folks just sit on the hill with binoculars and try to see what they can see. More often than not, impatience gets the best of them and they go on their way. There's something to be said for short attention spans."

By the time Thackery stopped talking, Minerva had slipped into the water, traversed the gentle waves, and slid below the surface. Russell's orientation was off to a good start.

Chapter 8

The olive-drab Volkswagen Iltis skidded to a stop in the gravel that fronted the church. While the German army surplus vehicle was far from new and required frequent attention, Comandante Delgado felt it added to his air of authority. It had been confiscated in lieu of taxes owed by a now-defunct charter business, and the policeman had a mechanic who would keep it running in exchange for the constabulary not looking into automotive parts that often went missing from unattended vehicles. Such recompense was actually rare for Delgado who almost always preferred cash for his thinly veiled protection racket that masqueraded as enhanced security. In Retiro de Santos, if one made money one paid money for what would normally be considered standard police practices. Those that didn't pay often found their establishments vandalized. It was cheaper to bear the cost of being left alone, rather than foot the bill for recurring busted doors, broken shutters, and missing merchandise. Delgado didn't regard his tactics as a protection scam. He rationalized that it was simply a remunerative bonus that moneyed citizens rather than the local government chose to dispense.

Before the policeman could ascend the three steps leading to the entrance of the church, the front door opened and Father Alonso stepped outside.

"Comandante, it has been many Sundays since you graced our house of worship."

"You know what they say, Father. No rest for the weary."

"Some say no rest for the wicked."

"You would disparage me, Father?"

"I make a literary point, not a judgmental one."

"Well, crime doesn't stop for Sunday services, therefore neither do my responsibilities."

"Your primary responsibility is to your God, Comandante."

"No, that is your primary responsibility. Mine is to the citizens of Retiro de Santos."

"I guess we can agree to disagree for now, Comandante. What brings you by today?"

"I stay so busy, Father. It's hard to keep up with citizens coming and going. Recently I have been made aware that the Australian, Thackery, is leaving and an American is taking his place."

"The man who works for the World Conservation Organization? He is leaving?"

"You were not aware of this, Father?"

"No. Why should I be?"

"I thought he might have spoken to you. To get things off his chest, as they say. Individuals sometimes do that when they are making big changes in life, yes?"

"I suppose so. But he never came to church regularly. From time to time, I would see him in the pews. But not often. I don't even know if he is actually a Catholic?"

"Had he been, and had he spoken to you... say in confession, perhaps... then you would be duty bound not to repeat whatever he might have told you. Correct?"

"That is true, Comandante. Not relevant in this particular

situation, but true. Why do you ask about this Thackery? Do you suspect him of some crime? Is he running away to avoid responsibility of some sort?"

"Who can say why people do what they do? There is no current investigation. It is simply part of my job to know as · much as I can about everyone who comes to Retiro de Santos. And those who leave it."

"That can be a tall order, Comandante."

"No rest for the weary, Father."

"Ah… we are back to that again, are we? Weary or wicked? I suppose time will tell. But, since you asked me a question, let me pose one to you?"

"If it is a quick one, Father. I have much to do today."

"Tell me, Comandante, is it a crime… legally, is it a crime to make someone do something they don't want to do?"

Delgado gave the priest a look of concern before answering. "That is a difficult question, Father. It depends on *what* one is being made to do. It depends on *who* is doing the doing and *who* is doing the making. I cannot answer correctly if I do not know these things."

"Suppose a father was going to make his daughter do something she did not want to do."

"Such as?"

"Such as working at Simone's."

"Father, you surprise me. How do you know of Simone's?"

"I frequently hear about it in confession. And like you, it is my job to watch over my flock."

"This father and daughter question is hard to answer. I suppose the father and the family are poor… and they need the money such work would bring?"

"*Sí*. But I was asking from a legal point of view, not an economic one."

"Well, the daughter must do what the father wants, until she becomes an adult. After that, she can do as she pleases."

"But what if she is not of age?"

"Not of age to be an adult? Or not of age for sexual consent?"

"The latter."

"How old is she?"

"Old enough to know that it is wrong and that she doesn't want to do it."

"But old enough to consent, yes? You of all people, Father, know that sex begins when it begins. Often much sooner here than in other parts of the world."

"That does not make it right?"

"You did not ask if it was right, only if it was legal."

"Legal and illegal is your business, Comandante. Right and wrong is mine."

"Then I'll leave you to your business, Father. And I will attend to mine. But do not expect me to get in the middle of family squabbles. I have enough to do already."

Chapter 9

Russell was getting used to being awakened each day by Bolivar, the coatimundi who had already decided to move his allegiance from Thackery to the American. The coati would hop silently on the cot, then get close enough to flap his ringed tail across Russell's nose or cheek. There was no way to misunderstand the message. It was time to get up.

The week seemed to fly by as the majority of time was spent going to and coming back from the beach, checking for new eggs, cleaning up hazards that sometimes washed ashore, and then returning to the cabin to go over Thackery's extensive notes that he kept in a journal he planned to leave with Russell.

Work didn't occupy every waking hour, however, and the two men also shared bits and pieces of their personal backgrounds as the days and nights passed. Thackery regaled his temporary roommate with his history of ribald adolescent adventures and frequent run-ins with kangaroos, dingoes, koalas, and more. Russell recounted his childhood on the plains, teachers, pals, and occasionally girlfriends from the past. Yet, when he was asked specifically why he decided to sign up with the WCO instead of immediately going into teaching, his answer was as non-specific as it had been when Delgado posed virtually the same question. Thackery didn't probe. He could tell Russell wanted to keep that particular subject vague, and he saw no benefit in pestering the American about it.

On the Thursday preceding the Saturday he was scheduled to leave, Thackery got off the phone and said, "Well, fancy that."

"Fancy what?" Russell asked.

"They're throwing us a piss-up."

"A what?"

"A piss-up… you know, a party."

"A party? What for? And who are they?"

"Apparently, it's to bid me a fond farewell and to welcome you. And *they* are a few of the Retiro de Santos upper-crusts and swells, with a smattering of hoi polloi thrown in just to spice things up."

"Were you expecting this? You didn't say anything about it."

"Out of the blue, mate. Had no idea anyone cared one way or the other. Maybe the WCO profile is increasing. Who's to say? But the drinks are free. The women are loose… or they will be after a few cold ones. And yours truly has never been one to look a gift horse in the mouth, as they say."

"So, when and where is this party to take place?"

"Tomorrow night at the palatial estate of Mr. Leland Bennett."

"And he is…?"

"A bloke I haven't crossed paths with all that often. He's one of the few landed gentry around here. Rumor has it, his family was a lot better off in the past. Though he still manages to get tipped hats, nodded heads, and hushed whispers when he graces the town square with his presence."

"Sounds interesting," Russell said. "So, we're going, I guess?"

"In style, mate. In style."

Chapter 10

Thackery showed up in sand-colored, starched safari garb, with creases and pleats pressed neatly. Russell wore a brown corduroy jacket with elbow patches, a black knit tie, blue button-down oxford shirt, and chinos. The two men blended in perfectly with the rest of the partygoers who were attired in everything from cargo shorts to evening wear. The crowd was a testament to incompatibility.

Having been there only long enough to secure a couple of drinks from the open bar, Thackery and Russell were about to begin milling when the American spotted a man coming their way. He was older, somewhere in his sixties, Russell guessed. The man's salt and pepper hair was combed straight back and due to its length, fell willy-nilly over the back collar of his white dinner jacket. His meticulously trimmed pencil mustache was spaced evenly between his nose and mouth. The dichotomy between his manicured facial hair and his almost unkempt mane mirrored the overall surroundings, Russell thought. He had noted upon their arrival that the spacious home carved into the side of a mountain was initially stunning, but the closer one came to the edifice itself, the more its age spots became apparent. There were hairline cracks in the supporting foundation. Columns on the huge veranda that looked out over the sea revealed peeling paint here and there. Though the roof shone brightly as the last of the sun hit its high-gloss, forest-green tiles, a few were broken and in one or two spots, missing altogether. Both the place and the people who now populated it gave Russell an initial feeling of decline. It was a feeling he didn't care for, so he kept it to himself. But he wondered if the man who was about to greet them was in some way a larger part of the fading glory that seemed to surround all present.

"Hello Thackery, nice to see you again," the man said before turning to Russell. "I'm Leland Bennett."

"Hello, Mr. Bennett. Thanks for having us. You have a beautiful home here."

"Indeed you do, Bennett," Thackery cut in. "Shame this is my first and last time to see it in person."

"Yes, the fault lies with me, I suppose. Don't have guests over as often as I used to. Perhaps tonight can make amends for my social malfeasance. As well as providing an opportunity for our newest inhabitant to meet some of his fellow citizens."

Russell identified the remnants of a British accent in Bennett's speech. "Are you English, Mr. Bennett?"

"In a manner of speaking," Bennett replied. "Born and raised there, but my family moved here when I was still rather young. To oversee the sugar cane plantation. Thought I'd jettisoned the last vestiges of the mother tongue, but I guess not. And please, call me Leland."

The three continued to engage in small talk for a few more seconds, then Bennett offered to introduce Russell to some of the other guests, at which point Thackery took his leave to chat up the closest female.

Russell wasn't particularly adept at remembering names.

After an initial introduction to this man or that couple, he'd frequently be unable to recall how to address the person he was talking to. But not being totally unskilled in the art of conversation, he'd always find a way to politely disengage without betraying his forgetfulness. Eventually, Bennett was approached by one of the servers who whispered something in his ear. Apologizing to Russell, he stepped away to attend to the man's concern. Then the American was approached by someone he'd met previously.

"Good evening, Mr. Russell."

"Comandante... Delgado, right?"

"Correct. We met in my office."

"Of course. Taking a break from your police duties this evening?"

"Not at all. I am always on call. I thought it appropriate to welcome you to Retiro de Santos with others from the community. But should I be needed elsewhere, my people know how to reach me."

"Certainly. I understand. And I appreciate you being here. It's always nice to see a face I've already seen before. Makes me feel a little less the stranger, you know."

"I do know what you mean. But you need not feel like an outsider, merely a newcomer, who will soon be a friend to many. I am sure."

"I hope so."

"Speaking of friends... have you and Mr. Thackery gotten along this week?"

"Oh yes. He's been great. I couldn't have asked for a nicer... bloke, as he would say, to learn from."

"And has he taught you much... about the beach, and other things?"

"Certainly about the beach. He's an excellent conservationist.

Not sure what you mean by other things?"

"Oh, simply about our village, our people, businesses, and other entities here."

"Not as much as I'd like. We just haven't had time. But I'm looking forward to finding out more about everything in the days ahead."

"Well, as you do so..."

Delgado didn't get to finish his sentence. He was interrupted by the village priest.

"*Hola*. I'm Father Alonso Tejeda. You must be Mr. Russell."

"Yes. I am. I take it you two know each other."

"Oh yes, the Padre and I have watched over our community for some time. In different ways, of course."

"That is true," Father Alonso began. "He legally. Me spiritually. Our methods differ, but often our goals are the same. The care of our people."

"Well, it's very nice to meet you, Father."

"So, tell me, Señor Russell, are you by chance Catholic?"

Russell was slow to answer, and when he did an unstated apology meandered through his words. "Well, yes and no. I mean, I was raised Catholic, but frankly, I've sort of fallen away from the church over the years. I actually don't attend mass very often."

"How often is not often?" The priest asked.

"Well... sort of like... never."

Father Alonso cocked his head, blinked, and said, "At least you are honest, my son. That is a beginning. And new beginnings are what this world offers every day. Especially for one such as you who is beginning a new physical life here. This would be a wonderful time for you to renew your spiritual life as well."

"You will have to forgive Father Alonso, Mr. Russell,"

Delgado interjected. "He never misses a chance to make what you Americans call, his sales pitch."

"It is not a pitch, Comandante. Merely a reminder that it is never too late to reconnect with the Savior and the church."

Before Russell had a chance to reply, a fragrance not unlike orange blossoms lightened the air as a female whirlwind swept into the middle of the trio, grabbed him by the arm, and said, "You two purveyors of penance and punishment have had this fellow long enough. Time for him to get to know a heathen or two. I'll bring him back in one piece. Maybe."

The policeman and the priest looked at each other, cocked their heads, and merely shrugged in compliance. This wasn't the first time Inez Munoz had made a grand entrance. With Russell in tow, she swept him across the room, past the bar where she scooped up two wine glasses and a bottle of white burgundy, then outside onto one of the veranda's loveseats. There, she began to fill each glass as Russell took a long look at the woman who had more or less kidnapped him in plain sight.

She had shoulder-length red hair that leaned toward purple except for the black roots that could have used a touch-up. Her brows were similarly colored and arched over green eyes that danced a little in the overhead light. Her nose was neither large nor small with a tip that tilted slightly to the left. When she handed him a glass of wine, he noticed her smile was a bit crooked and perhaps as playful as he had ever seen. Since at this point he could only guess, he put her somewhere in her mid-thirties. Older than him but certainly not too old. He couldn't help but continue his gaze down her one-piece pantsuit that accented appropriate curves, long legs, and gold shoes the same color as her hoop earrings.

"Like what you see?"

Russell embarrassed, looked up. "Ah… yeah. I mean, well, yes."

"I did, too. That's why I pulled you away from the cat and mouse."

"So, which is which?"

"Delgado cat. Father Alonso mouse."

"And you?"

"I'm Inez."

"I'm Russell. Stephen Russell."

"I know. That's why I came tonight. I like meeting new people."

"I'm really not a new person. Just new to Retiro de Santos."

"I know that as well. The new WCO man, right?"

"Right. But how did you know?"

"Leland told me. You're the reason for the party. I come to all of Leland's parties."

"Gives a lot of them, does he?"

"Not as many as he used to."

"Why is that?"

"Have to ask him."

Russell said apologetically, "You're probably not going to believe this… but in the short time we've been together, I've already forgotten your name."

"I'm that forgettable, huh?"

"No. No. In fact, there's a good chance you may be unforgettable. It's just that I'm terrible at remembering names."

"Okay… then focus… my name is Inez."

"Inez. Right. It would help me remember your name if I knew more about you."

"I'm a painter."

"You mean, like houses, or buildings?"

"No. I paint pictures. Portraits. Still lifes. Landscapes and such."

"Oh, you're an artist?"

"Well, that's up to others, isn't it?"

"What do you mean?"

"I mean, I paint. So I'm a painter. I call myself a painter. I don't call myself an artist. That's not for me to decide. That's for those who see my paintings to decide. If they call me an artist, then I am. If I call myself an artist, I'm simply flattering myself."

"And you don't care to do that?"

"Actually, I do. But I work hard at not doing it."

"Do you show your work? Is it in a gallery here or somewhere else?"

"It's a bit of everywhere, really. There's a gallery in the main square that has some of my work. As well as a couple of cafés. The hotel has one large painting."

"Oh, I see, the tourist trade. They're your main clients?"

"Well they are and they aren't. Yes, they buy some of my paintings at the gallery. But very few. Mostly they want the caricatures I offer for infinitely less money. They'd rather have a sketch of themselves than rotting pairs captured on canvas. The former is approximately one-tenth the price of the latter, which I sell a lot of when the weather's good and people are in town. I make up in volume what I lose in margin."

"You sound like a businesswoman as well as a painter."

"One has to be from time to time. But the fact is I'm also one of those god-awful trust fund babies. My parents left me rather well off. However, I choose to live the starving artist's life. 'Starving' being a relative term, of course. It's much more bohemian and if things go badly, I can always fall back on money that's just sitting around making more money. But enough about me. Let's talk about you."

"Why?"

"Because I want to. And because I have the wine."

"Okay," Russell said. "Refill my glass and we'll talk about me."

Inez refilled his glass and hers.

After touching glasses and each taking a drink, Russell said, "All right. What would you like to know?"

"What's with people like you and Thackery?"

"What do you mean?"

"I mean, why spend all your time looking into and after turtles, for God's sake?"

"I can't speak for Thackery."

"Don't expect you to. But what about you?"

"I think it's a good thing to do?"

"What's so good about it?"

"Well, for one," Russell began, "sea turtles have been around since the dinosaurs. Literally a hundred million years. I believe it's a good thing to help keep them around even longer."

"Know a lot about sea turtles do you?"

"This and that."

"Okay, enlighten me, then."

"What would you like to know?"

"Well, they're all more or less the same, right? Slow walkers with hard shells who scrunch their heads and legs in when trouble comes their way, right?"

"Not really. There are flatback turtles, green turtles, hawksbill turtles, loggerhead turtles, olive ridley turtles, and leatherback turtles... whose shells are not like hardened bone. Rather, they're made up of a tough, leathery substance. Basically, a rubbery shell of cartilage. And, loggerhead can't actually retract their heads under their shells."

"That's sad. Guess they have to just fend for themselves with their heads out and about like the rest of us, huh?"

"They do okay. You certainly wouldn't want one to clamp onto you."

"Ever had that experience?"

"No. Luckily we're a lot quicker than they are."

"All those different types you mentioned... tend to mix and mate a lot, do they?"

"Not really. They pretty much stick to their own kind."

"Not sexually experimental, huh?"

"Not particularly. In fact, sometimes, they don't even need sex, as we know it, to become *gravid*."

"*Gravid*?"

"Pregnant."

"Whoa. Gravid without sex. I mean where's the fun in that?"

"Fun doesn't play a big part," Russell went on. "In fact, they're less than enamored with relationships. Males never actually come ashore. They prefer the open sea, cold water, and anywhere from four to seven hours at a time under the surface. Though they can't stay there forever. They do have to come up for air every now and then. And the females, well, some might consider them less than ideal mothers. Once a female is with eggs, the incubation period lasts about sixty to seventy-five days. The mother will only lay her eggs in darkness. And once she has, the eggs are left to hatch on their own. It's totally up to the hatchlings themselves to make their way to the sea."

"Orphans from the get-go, huh?"

"That's why we try to help. And it gets tougher every year," Russell continued. "The mother may literally cross the Pacific to return to a particular nesting beach she prefers. But now she faces more problems than ever."

"Such as?"

"Encroaching beach erosion, all the continuing commercial

development, fishermen operating out of bounds, debris in the ocean, trash on shore."

"So, people like you and Thackery…?"

"Promote more responsible fishing practices. Encourage fewer mega nets. Identify marine protective areas so people will stay away. Use satellite I.D. tags to monitor migration patterns."

"And you wander up and down the beach a lot."

"We do. In some areas, just walking up and down the beach picking up trash, filling in holes, removing sand castles that keep hatchlings from making it out to sea… those seemingly little things enable more hatchlings to survive."

"You're the good guys, huh?"

Russell realized he had gotten a little carried away. "I'd like to think so," he said, haltingly.

Then, as if from out of nowhere, Inez asked, "Would you like to kiss me?"

Russell, caught totally off guard, hesitated before answering.

"If you have to think about it, that means you probably don't."

"Oh, no. It's not that. It's just… well, I mean… yes. Yes, I would like to kiss you?"

Both leaned forward until their lips met. Not once, but twice. Then a third time.

Inez spoke first. "Bet you'd like to see more of my work, wouldn't you? Want to go to my place?"

"That would be nice," Russell answered. "But I need to let Thackery know."

"He's a big boy. He'll figure it out."

They left their glasses but took the bottle with them as they walked down the steps of the veranda and headed for the side of the house.

"Do you have a car?" Russell asked.

"No. But I have a scooter."

"Then, lead the way."

"If you haven't noticed, that's what I've been doing."

Chapter 11

As morning light spilled through the louvered shutters, across the floor, and over the bare bottom lying next to him, Russell reflected, in the parlance of the day, that he had certainly gotten lucky the night before. An unplanned, unexpected, totally awesome sexual romp with an attractive and witty woman was not something he envisioned when he and Thackery... oh, no. Thackery, Russell remembered. He was supposed to see him off this morning. Damn, he almost said out loud. He must have slept right through it. Throwing the sheet that covered him aside, he bolted from the bed to make a quick run to the bathroom. Then he recalled that he wasn't sure where it was. He wasn't in his cabin. He was in Inez's walk-up. Surrounded by easels, canvases, brushes, paint cans, and more. Standing naked in the middle of the room he was having a hard time focusing.

"It's the door on your left," Inez said from her still supine position in bed.

"Oh, thanks," Russell quickly responded. "I'm late. I'm supposed to be somewhere."

"Could have fooled me. I thought you were somewhere."

Returning from the bathroom, Russell began to rapidly search the room for various articles of clothing, hastily putting each piece on as he found it and apologizing simultaneously.

"So sorry to run like this. But I told Thackery I'd see him off this morning. He's supposed to be picked up at Punto Alvidado cove and taken to the ship."

"How were you going to get there?"

"The hotel rental car was hired. I bet I've missed it."

"Take my scooter," Inez suggested. "The key's on that table over there."

Shoes on but untied, socks in his jacket pocket, and tie looped around his neck like a scarf, Russell hurried to the table, grabbed the keys, and almost headed for the stairs. Then he spun around and quickly returned to the bed where he leaned down and held Inez by both bare shoulders.

"Listen… thanks for last night. It was wonderful," he said.

"It was?"

"You mean it wasn't?"

"No, I don't mean that," she countered. "It's just that it's so damn early and you have to run."

"Oh, yeah. Have to run. I'll bring the scooter back this afternoon."

"Whenever," she said. "No rush."

Then Russell pulled her close for a quick kiss, let her go, and bolted for the door. Inez fell back on the bed, pulled the sheet over her head, and was already sliding toward sleep again by the time Russell raced down the stairs, threw open the door, and slammed it shut on his way out.

*   *   *

The cove at Punto Alvidado was as beautiful as Russell

remembered it upon his arrival. But there was no one on shore waiting to be picked up. There was no dinghy at the beach or making its way back to the ship. In fact, there was no ship either. *Damn*, Russell said to himself. *I did miss it. Unless I'm early instead of late.* He wore no watch and wasn't sure of the time. So he quickly turned the scooter around and headed down the mountain toward town, thinking that if he was early, he'd pass the rental car on the way. He didn't. No cars were on the road between his descent and the village. He immediately motored to the hotel. The rental car was sitting out front. Russell turned off the scooter and went inside to see if the car had picked up its passenger, taken him to the drop-off point, and already returned. He learned it hadn't. The clerk told him that the customer who had requested the car was not at his residence when the driver went to pick him up, and that no one had come in that morning seeking a ride to Punto Alvidado. Russell found the whole thing confusing. He was sure Thackery had told him that the rental car would come to their cabin, pick him up, and take him to the cove. The plan was for Russell to accompany him, see Thackery off, then the rental would drop Russell off at the cabin on its way back to town. But apparently, none of that had happened. Something was definitely amiss. So he got back on the scooter to drive to the cabin he had shared with Thackery for the past week.

When Russell arrived, he saw two vehicles parked on the virtually non-existent shoulder of the road near the cabin. One was an odd-looking, green military-type auto, the other appeared to be some sort of elongated station wagon. There were no people beside either, so Russell pulled the scooter off the road near the limestone walkway, parked it, took the path up to the cabin, opened the unlocked front door, and went inside. The place was empty. No Thackery. No drivers of the other vehicles. Not even Bolivar, unless the coati was hiding under the bed or in the closet. Walking to the rear of the cabin, he then stepped outside. After a second or two, he thought he heard voices coming from the path that led to the beach. He immediately started down and had not gone far when he heard even louder voices coming toward him. He knew there was little room to pass on the path, so he stopped abruptly and waited for the voices to arrive.

Soon Delgado, and two men carrying a stretcher between them, appeared. There was something on the stretcher, beneath a sheet. The policeman saw Russell as the procession continued up the grade. He motioned for the men to put the stretcher down and rest for a moment. Then he walked up to where Russell was standing.

"Do you know what has happened, here?" Delgado asked.

"No. I just got here. I was running late. What's that?"

"Mister Russell, I regret to inform you that Neil Thackery is dead."

He heard the comandante but hoped he hadn't. "Dead? What do you mean? He was all set to leave this morning. I was to go along part way and wish him bon voyage... but I've been running late. Dead? Did you say, dead? You can't be serious."

"Come with me," the policeman replied. Then he walked to where the two men had placed the stretcher on the ground between them. With a wave of his hand, he indicated for the man in the rear to pull the sheet back so Russell could see. There was no doubt. It was Thackery. The corpse had major bruises near his eyes and mouth that had turned purple and yellow. There were cuts and scratches on the remainder of his face as well. A large knot protruded from one side of his head and dried blood had hardened around it.

"My God. What happened?"

"Thackery must have slipped and fallen down the hill," Delgado said. "His clothes are wrinkled and torn, We found him near the bottom."

"Slipped? He wouldn't have slipped," Russell said adamantly. "He knew this path like the back of his hand. Went down and up it all the time."

"Perhaps this time was different," Delgado suggested. "Perhaps he was not up to it this time."

"Up to it? What do you mean?"

"When Thackery left Señor Bennett's reception last night, he was heavily intoxicated. I, along with others saw him. I believe it was some time after you left."

"But, why... why would he even be out here. He was going to leave this morning. There was no reason for him to go back down to the beach."

"Who knows? Perhaps it was something sentimental. Perhaps he desired to see the place by moonlight. Or he wanted to see a sunrise here for the last time. Who knows?"

"Wait. Wait a minute," Russell shook his head. "If he wanted to see the sunrise, why was he still in the clothes he wore last night?"

Delgado looked at the American from top to bottom. "Why are you?"

"I... I just can't believe he'd fall. He knew this path so well."

"Too much liquor. Too little caution. A tragedy indeed. But accidents happen. I cannot tell you why," the policemen said. "That is more in Father Alonso's area of expertise."

"But... if he tumbled down the hill, that wouldn't necessarily kill him."

"You saw the large bruise on his head, Mr. Russell. We found a boulder on the way down with blood on it. Hitting such a rock at a high rate of speed. That could easily have done it."

"I just can't believe it," Russell said. Then as he rubbed his own forehead, something else came to mind. "But what are you and they... what are you... I mean when did you get here? How did you know about this?"

"A call was made to the police station," Delgado answered.

"A call? From whom?"

"We do not know. The caller would not give a name. Just told us there was a body along this path and disconnected."

"But, why would someone do that... not give their name, or wait for you to arrive?"

"Often, people do not like to be around tragedy. And perhaps even more often, they do not want to be involved with anything that might attract the police."

"My God. I just can't believe he's dead. Or that he tripped and fell. He was like a mountain goat on this path. Where's that boulder that you spoke of? The one with the blood?"

Before Delgado could answer, thunder cracked, and rain began to spill from the sky in dime-sized drops. In moments, the dirt beneath them was turning to mud. Brush and tree leaves were splattered and shaken by the wind. The men themselves were getting soaked, while rocks big and small were being washed clean.

"Not now," Delgado shouted. "We must get the body out of here."

Russell wasn't sure what to do. At that moment, he wasn't sure of anything. So he simply turned and led them back to the cabin.

Chapter 12

Days have a way of turning into weeks. Weeks have a way of dulling pain and fogging memory. Russell was experiencing a little of both. He had not known Thackery that long, but in the short time they spent together, he had looked upon him as a friend as well as a co-worker, and Russell didn't make friends easily or keep them for long. That's one of the reasons the WCO job appealed to him. He could perform his duties on his own and be as secluded or social as he wanted to be. Though he knew the former was much more likely. It had been for some time.

The Australian's funeral was perfunctory. As the only holy man in town, Father Alonso presided over a graveside service. Thackery's body was put to rest in a small cemetery near the church. The fact that he may or may not have been Catholic was overlooked. The living chose not to make an issue of it; the dead are without prejudice. Before the ceremony, Russell had gone down to the beach to see if the giant leatherback Thackery had named Minerva was nearby. He saw no sign of her. But somehow he felt she knew.

The service itself was sparsely attended. No relatives came

from far away. No one, other than Russell, was sent from the WCO. Delgado was there, more officially than sentimentally. The hotel manager, a couple of café and bar owners were present, as was a well-dressed Black woman with white hair that Russell heard Leland Bennett address as Simone. No one introduced themselves or shared remembrances. Simply showing up was apparently in and of itself respect enough. Such proceedings do give one pause, however, whether the occasion is flamboyant or underwhelming. Russell wondered if his own passing would one day be similarly mechanical.

Inez Munoz did not attend. When she and Russell spoke on his return of her scooter she let him know that funerals were impossible for her. The whole idea of burial or cremation, for that matter, was something she just couldn't accept. Readily admitting it was a terrible failing of reality on her part, she still insisted that's just the way it was, and the only funeral she ever intended on attending was her own. Adding she'd do what she could to avoid that one as well.

While the two had not gone out of their way to avoid one another since their initial night together, neither had overtly suggested repeating it. Russell realized it was ludicrous to feel guilty about separating himself from Thackery on the last night of his life, but guilt came easy to the American. He had no idea why Inez had not mentioned that night nor any potential one in their future. If she had not enjoyed it, he wasn't in a hurry to hear why. If she was embarrassed about initiating the whole thing, she had certainly never shown it. He doubted that she was concerned about getting overly involved. So he decided he'd just let events take their own course and if a moment presented itself to be as spontaneous as they were before, well, it would happen or it wouldn't. He'd wait and see.

*   *   *

The day dawned with an orange sky and continued to brighten. Russell was taking the back path to the beach as he always did now, unless wind and rain caused the descent to be so treacherous that it made more sense to go the long way around. Halfway down he saw what appeared to be someone sitting just off the path, partially hidden by the thick undergrowth. The individual's back was turned to Russell and the long black hair that cascaded down indicated the onlooker was most likely female. Not wanting to frighten her, he called out as he walked. "¡*Hola*! *Buenos días.*"

Her head spun around at the sound and she quickly rose to her feet. She looked as if she was about to bolt and run away. Russell didn't want her to accidentally stumble or fall.

"Ah, careful. ¡*Ten cuidado*! It's very steep here. *Es... muy empinado.*"

"I can speak English," came back the cautious reply from the girl whose eyes were as dark as her hair.

"That's good. So can I." Russell's joke missed its mark, but the friendliness in his voice and the smile on his face eased the young girl's trepidation. She held her ground.

Walking to her slowly, he extended his hand and said, "I'm Stephen Russell. I live back there in the cabin. What's your name?"

She looked at his outstretched hand. It took a moment for her to realize that he was doing what so many of the foreigners did with one another. She reached out and shook it.

"I am Elena."

"That's a lovely name. Almost as lovely as you. What are you doing here, Elena?"

"Just looking. I watch the beach. Is so pretty here."

"Yes, the view is great. But it can be dangerous along this path if you're not used to it."

"I know it well. I come here often."

"You do. I've never seen you here."

"I stay off the path. Out of the way. I do not go to the beach. I know we are not allowed."

"That's because it's a protected area. Too many people could cause harm and make it impossible for the sea turtles to come and go as they should."

"You are the new tortoise man?"

"Yes. I am."

"I only watch. I mean no harm."

"I'm sure that's true," Russell replied.

"Sometimes... down there... a rock moves. I have seen that."

"You have? Then you see very well."

Russell liked the girl immediately. Her innocence was obvious, as was her curiosity.

"I'm going down to check some things now. Would you like to come with me?"

"Is permitted?"

"Not always. But since I'm in charge... it's permitted today."

"*Sí, señor.* I mean... yes. Yes, I would, Mr....?"

"Russell. But since I'm calling you Elena. Why don't you call me Stephen."

"Is permitted?"

"It is."

Chapter 13

The Hotel's restaurant was less than full. It wasn't the height of tourist season. A few couples were scattered here and there. The couple by the window, however, weren't really a couple, and they definitely weren't tourists. Leland Bennett had extended an invitation for breakfast and Simone had accepted. She seldom turned down Bennett's invitations. To her, he was still a vestige of what used to be the privileged class in Retiro de Santos. Those whose presence was deemed more valuable to the village than the majority of inhabitants. Bennett's position was achieved through wealth. His family owned and ran the sugar cane plantation that provided more paying jobs than any other form of local employment. Over the years, the size, yield, and output of the plantation had continually decreased. It was debatable whether that was due to the vicissitudes of nature or the ineptitude of Bennett's management after his parents died. Whichever was the case, even in its suboptimal status it remained the primary source of wages for men and women with strong backs, nimble hands, and little or no education.

Simone had joined the aristocratic fringe of Retiro de Santos via an entirely different route. Her ticket to entry was not family, but beauty. The offspring of a passing African sailor and a local peasant girl, Simone grew into a cocoa-skinned temptress with eyes like black pearls and a form carved from sin itself. Barely adolescent before being taken advantage of by a local farmer, she turned degradation into determination and decided to exploit the economic opportunity in the urges of boys and the lust of men. Through trial, error, and perseverance, her business acumen rose in lockstep with her erotic techniques. Over the years she became not only a supplier of sexual favors but also a recruiter of young women willing to use their feminine attributes as an antidote to poverty. Now in her fifth decade, she was the owner and sole proprietor of a home that congenially housed her personnel and cheerily hosted both locals and visitors.

"More coffee?" Bennett asked.

"I could use another cup," Simone answered.

Catching the eye of the waitress across the room, he raised his cup and it was responded to with a nod of understanding.

"Only be a moment," he said.

"Patience is a virtue," she replied. "Perhaps the one I practice best."

"I noticed you barely touched your breakfast. Didn't care for it?"

"It was fine. But at my age, one must remain more cognizant of calories than ever."

"Simone, your lovely form has not declined in the least."

"Nor has your flattery, Leland. Sincere or otherwise. But I appreciate the gesture."

The waitress arrived, refilled their coffee cups, then walked away.

"A pretty girl," Bennett said.

"Passing fair," Simone commented. "I wasn't sure you still

took note of such things… having not seen you at my place for some time."

"The demands of overseeing a difficult business. And age's assault on libido."

"You're not that old, Leland."

"Perhaps not. But getting older every day."

"Maybe all you need is more variety."

"You might have a point. There's a reason for the cliché, I guess. Any new employees I'm not familiar with?"

"I'm looking into one now. The Esperaza girl. A real beauty. And just beginning to blossom."

"Experienced?"

"I don't think so. But that's what I'm for."

"Expensive?"

"Of course. But that's what you or some other well-to-do client is for."

"Oh, by the way, my apologies for not saying hello at Thackery's funeral."

"Don't give it a second thought. I'm used to being kept at arm's length in public gatherings."

"Wasn't particularly well attended, was it?"

"One or two of the girls wanted to come, but I discouraged it."

"Was he a regular customer?"

"From time to time. No particular pattern."

"Did he ever talk much about his job or the WCO?"

"Few of my customers come to talk."

"I know, but your well-stocked bar and pleasant company often lend themselves to conversation, I would imagine. And he was quite a garrulous fellow."

"On occasion, he would comment on the good works his organization was involved in. More often than not he'd ramble more about endangered species. Suppose he didn't realize that he had become one."

"What makes you say that?" Bennett asked.

"Oh, just thinking out loud," Simone answered. "I mean, do you really believe he accidentally fell and killed himself?"

"He was drunk at the party. Certainly drunk enough to stumble virtually anywhere. And on that rough terrain, well."

"I'm sure you're right. Conservationists can be as reckless as the rest of us."

"And what about this new fellow, this Russell? Has he had occasion to visit?"

"No. He hasn't. But he's a pretty young man. Perhaps he finds satisfaction elsewhere."

"Perhaps. But young men and their desires… well, you know what I mean."

"I do indeed. I'm sure he'll eventually find his way."

"Well, should he do so anytime soon, I'd be interested to hear if he has anything to say about the WCO's plans."

"Plans?"

"You know…any input regarding the future of the beach sanctuary… anything like that?"

"And just why would that be of interest to you, Leland?"

He took a sip of coffee before responding, more to frame his response than assuage his thirst. "Like all of us who care about Retiro de Santos, I want to keep up with the people and organizations that affect our little part of the world. Doing so enables me to become a stronger advocate, when and if decisions have to be made. You know it is often said that knowledge is power."

"Knowledge is a good thing, certainly. The more one knows, the more one can profit from knowing what others may not. And making a profit is a particularly good thing. Is it not, Leland?"

"I have found it to be."

"As have I. So I will keep my ears open should Mr. Russell choose to visit my establishment. And I assume, Leland, if there's something going on that might profit us both… you'll share what you know as well."

"Of course, Simone. As major contributors to Retiro de Santos's past, who is more deserving than us to be part of its future?"

"No one."

Chapter 14

Bolivar was becoming as fond of Elena as he was of Russell. He enjoyed mussing her long raven locks with his paws and tail. She had begun to steal away as often as she could to spend more time with this man who was kind enough to share what he knew of marine life and more. She constantly asked him about America, and he would often teasingly test her recall of the knowledge he'd imparted about everything from historic migration patterns to Hollywood movie stars. She could recount all she had learned of both, equally well.

One morning on the beach they came upon a circle of upturned sand. He spotted it ahead of them and put his hand on her shoulder.

"Stop. Look there, Elena, can you see that indentation?"

"Yes. Yes, I see it. Is that…"

"It is. Eggs have been laid there. I will have to watch it closely to see that it's not disturbed."

"How long before the babies come?"

"I can't be sure. Could be a month or more. I'll just have to check each day."

"Will the animals stay away?"

"I hope so. I'll do what I can to make sure the area around here is not disturbed."

"It is not fair. It is terrible that dogs or other animals might kill them."

"You're right. But many things in life and nature are unfair. Animals scrounge for food wherever they can find it. They survive purely on instinct. Hunger is not right or wrong for them. It's just hunger. That's why those of us who know the difference need to help whenever we can."

Elena turned away and spoke as much to herself as to Russell. "Some people know right from wrong, and still do wrong."

"Yes, some people do, I guess. And some wind up doing wrong even when they're trying to do what's right."

It was as if the two had been talking to themselves even as they conversed with one another. But then her reflections turned to the present.

"My father wants me to do wrong," Elena said under her breath.

Lost in his own train of thought, Russell said, "Sometimes it seems impossible to know why things happen as they do."

Hearing no response to what she'd said, Elena announced, "I have to go now, to help at home."

Russel also snapped back to the moment. "I'll walk you back up the hill. Need to get some things from the cabin anyway."

Neither said anything as they walked, both adrift in their own contemplations. When they approached the shack, Bolivar raced out to meet them and jumped on Elena's shoulder. She let him stay. Entering from the rear, they quickly realized they were not alone when they heard a voice before they saw who it was coming from.

"You always leave your front door unlocked?"

Beer in hand, Inez was sitting in a chair with her leg draped over one of its arms.

"Glad you found the refreshments," Russell said. "Had I known you were coming, I would have stocked something more appropriate."

"Just happened to be motoring by. Thought I'd stop and say hello."

Russell looked from Inez to Elena, quickly remembered his manners, and started to introduce them. "Inez, this is Elena Esperaza. Elena, this is—"

"I know who she is," Elena cut in. "She's the lady who draws pictures of the tourists. I have seen you at the hotel. Your pictures are very pretty. Sometimes funny, too."

"*Most* of those pictures are funny," Inez replied, "but don't tell the tourists. And none are as pretty as you. Maybe I could paint your portrait one day."

"Oh, that would be wonderful. But I have to go now, or I will get in trouble for being late. It was very nice to meet you."

"You, too, love," Inez replied, as Elena hurried out the front door. The artist then turned to Russell and said, "So, robbing the cradle now, huh?"

"No. Definitely not. Elena's a great kid. She cares a lot about the beach and marine life. I hope she has a chance to keep learning about it."

"And why wouldn't she?"

"I don't know. It just feels like she has a lot on her mind. Seems troubled, you know. But apparently, she doesn't want to talk about it."

"Maybe she just wants to hear you talk. Maybe she wants to hear you talk about more than turtles."

"Look," Russell said, "the kid's a teenager."

"And you've forgotten what teenagers think about most?"

"That's what teenage *boys* think about. Not girls."

"Wow. I didn't realize you were brought up in the Victorian age."

"She's a good kid and, believe me, we're only friends. Let's leave it at that, okay?"

"Okay. So, the real question is… are you just going to stand there and let me drink this beer alone? There's more in the fridge. I noticed when I got this one."

Russell responded with a comically insincere apology. "How rude of me. It wouldn't be hospitable to let you drink alone, would it? I'll join you."

As he walked into the kitchen to secure a bottle for himself, Inez rose and followed, saying, "I wasn't just riding by. I came out to see you because I actually wanted to see you."

"It's sort of taken a while, hasn't it?"

"Well, that's the pot calling the kettle black. I haven't heard from you either."

Russell took a swig of his beer before admitting, "The truth is, I was worried that you hadn't… you know… enjoyed our time together that much. So I didn't… well I just thought—"

"You thought I was a slut who only wanted a one-night stand. You thought I was a bitch who wouldn't even go to Thackery's funeral. You thought I was some cougar who just toyed with men and tossed them away."

"I didn't think any of that. And you're too young to be a cougar."

"Oooh. That's a lovely thing to say, that last bit. Oh well, you told me your truth, now I'll tell you mine. I was pretty gobsmacked with the night we spent together. I didn't tell you that because I didn't want it to go to your head. And I didn't want you to think I was that easy. Though… that particular night, I guess I was. But it wasn't like I was just looking for anyone. There was something about you. Something that made the night and the drinks and everything feel great. So I just went for it. Then I spent the next few weeks thinking maybe I had come on way too strong. I do that sometimes, you know?"

"You? Come on too strong? Never."

They both chuckled. Then Russell continued. "Well, we could always do some sort of a reset, couldn't we? I mean, we've laid our cards on the table. We could always just start over from scratch. Get to know one another better. Go out on a date, maybe."

"That's true. We could do that." Inez answered. "Or... we could just finish our beers, jump in the sack, and hump like minks."

Without hesitation, Russell replied, "Right plan. Wrong order. We'll finish our beers later."

Chapter 15

She had never argued with her father before. Until this moment it had been unthinkable that she would dare to verbally disagree, much less defy him with others around. But as her siblings watched and said nothing, and her mother—long since acquainted with the futility of trying to change her husband's mind—turned her face to the beans on the fire, Elena would not be silent.

"I won't do it. I won't."

"You will do as I say. And I will hear no more of it."

"But I can find other ways to make money."

"Not as much. Not nearly as much."

"I can ask at the hotel again."

"They don't need more maids."

"I can work the sugar cane fields."

"The wages are too small."

"I can ask Señor Russell to pay me for help with the tortoises."

"*Eso es estúpido*. He needs no help."

"I could—"

"No."

"But—"

"No."

"I—"

"Enough!"

His shout seemed to rattle the walls of their shanty. Now even her brothers looked away and acted as if they were intricately involved in something else, anything else.

"I have talked to the mistress of that house," her father said. "We have come to an understanding. I will hear no more about it. No more."

She would have run to her room if she had one. But she didn't. Just a mat set apart from the others. So there she retreated, turned to the wall, and did everything she possibly could to keep her sobs silent.

Chapter 16

As dinner parties go, it was a rather intimate gathering. Bennett had told Russell he was just having a few friends over. The American had yet to visit Simone's since she and Bennett breakfasted two weeks earlier. The pair thought perhaps he was too new, too shy, or too uninterested in women to venture into her establishment. Neither the plantation owner nor the madam knew that Russell's physical needs were being more than met by Inez Munoz, who was also invited. Bennett felt that she was bohemian enough to offset the more predictable banter from the two remaining guests that filled out the sextet, Comandante Delgado and Father Alonso.

Over aperitifs, the conversation began as most tête-à-têtes do with references to the weather, which was wet, and the wine, which was dry. It quickly segued into the recent demise of Thackery with Bennett, Simone, and Delgado regretting the fact that tragic accidents are unfortunately a part of life, Father Alonso again reminding everyone that the Lord moves in mysterious ways, Inez advocating for living every day of life as if it were one's last, and Russell's continuing inability to fully accept the fact that misstep alone led to Thackery's death.

After dinner, brandy moved them into both more practical and philosophical realms.

"So, Mr. Russell," Delgado asked, "have you become acquainted with Retiro de Santos's opportunities for rest and relaxation, or like so many of your countrymen, are you one of these… what is it called… workaholics."

"I try to strike a balance between work and leisure when I can," Russell answered.

"Though I don't believe you've visited my club yet," Simone said.

Russell responded, "That's true. But I've heard some in the square say nice things about it."

"I bet you have," Inez quickly interjected.

Before she had a chance to continue, Bennett added, "Yes, Simone's club is one of our village's most sophisticated diversions. Virtually everyone goes there at some time or another."

"Virtually every male." Inez clarified.

"Except for Father Alonso, of course," Simone added. "The good padre keeps his distance from temptation."

"As should we all," the priest said.

"Father," Simone continued, "I only provide that which is demanded. Were it not found in my club, it would be sought elsewhere."

"And we wouldn't want such activity on our streets and in our alleyways, would we, Comandante?" Bennett added.

"Indeed not," Delgado responded. "The citizens wouldn't stand for it, and the refined level of tourists to whom Retiro de Santos caters would find it off-putting as well."

"You must be running into a different level of tourist than I am," Inez quipped.

"Still," Bennett said, "a place for everything and everything in its place is probably an apt profundity for adult recreation."

"And religion, too, right, Father?" Simone's question was meant to be rhetorical but the priest answered anyway.

"I leave my sermons at the pulpit, but I give my advice and council wherever it is sought."

"I hand mine out whether it's sought or not," Inez joked.

"One of your most engaging qualities," Russell blurted, along with an involuntary smile that prompted the same from her, plus inquiring looks from the rest of their tablemates.

Getting closer to the point of the evening, Bennett asked, "So, Stephen, just how are those migrant sea turtles of yours?"

"Well, so far, so good. Of course, they're certainly not mine. They belong to each other and the world around us."

"Of course they do. And did Thackery, rest his soul, do a good job of... I believe you once referred to it as orientation. Did he adequately fill you in on what was needed and how things should be done?"

"He did, Leland. He was very thorough."

Father Alonso spoke. "I would imagine that you have to deal with a myriad of things to help keep them safe. Particularly in bad weather, yes?"

"Well, nature has taught them to deal with weather and the world around them. It's really us... people, you know... who wind up threatening them the most."

"Surely no one sets out to harm them," Simone suggested.

"Malicious intent? No. None that I've seen," Russell answered. "It's more thoughtlessness than anything else. Trash on the beach and in the water, things left behind on the hillside that eventually end up down below. It all becomes obstacles and impediments to nesting... and survival of the hatchlings."

Bennett continued addressing Russell. "As you say, nature has conditioned them over the ages. Certainly, they must have adapted... or learned to adjust to the human factor also. As more people populate more areas, the tortoise simply moves on, does it not?"

"There are fewer and fewer places to go," Russell answered. "Plus, over the centuries they've become hardwired to take certain routes to certain places and to return to where they came from."

"Time marches on," Delgado injected. "As the most intelligent of the species, human beings are destined to occupy more and more of our planet. One would think that nature... or perhaps, God... as Father Alonso would have us believe... has ways of making sure that adaptation by the lower life forms will continue to be accomplished."

"By making us the most intelligent," Father Alonso began, "God has also given us the responsibility to care for those who cannot always take care of themselves."

"An appropriate reminder, Father," Bennett began, "but such responsibility extends to our own species as well, does it not?"

"Obviously."

"Well... simply extrapolating for the purpose of conversation... could one not say that the particular stretch of beach that protects the sea creatures could protect even more human beings?"

"How so?" Russell asked before Father Alonso had a chance to.

"Again, just theorizing," Bennett said. "The beauty of that stretch of beach is without peer. If it were say, developed... you know... by some hospitality corporation or some real estate conglomerate... think of the economic opportunity it could provide for the human inhabitants of Retiro de Santos. Such work requires human labor for construction, followed by even more labor for maintenance and operation. Labor begets compensation... which means gainful employment for perhaps hundreds of people in Retiro de Santos. People who barely have enough to feed their families now. Would not the needs of our own people equal, or perhaps exceed, the needs of the turtle and its brethren?"

"Human encroachment has already put so many species in peril," Russell answered. "Is it right to continue it? Shouldn't the focus be more on *cohabitation*? Man and animal living in harmony."

"Depends on whom one asks," Delgado answered.

"That's true," Simone said. "The environmentalist, like Mr. Russell, might have one answer, whereas a poverty-stricken peasant might have another."

"And let's not forget those who might *profit* from fewer turtles and more hotels and condos," Inez inserted.

"Which would include artists and others who cater to tourists, yes?" Delgado asked, already knowing the answer.

"Touché, Comandante," Inez replied.

"So, Father," Simone quizzed. "In Leland's hypothetical world of help for the people or help for the beasts… which side would God come down on?"

"I make it a point never to speak for God," Father Alonso answered, "rather to simply repeat what he has told us. 'Let us make man in Our image, after Our likeness: and let him have dominion over the fish of the sea, over the fowl of the air, over the cattle, and over all the earth and everything that creeps upon the earth.'"

Inez injected, "But didn't he also say, 'Whoever is righteous has regard for the life of the beast'?"

"My dear," Father Alonso replied, "I did not know you were familiar with the scriptures."

"There is much about me that you, and others, do not know, Father. Frankly, that's the way I like it."

"A woman of mystery," Simone said. "There are so few of us in Retiro de Santos."

"And we are the recipients of your company tonight. How fortunate we males are," Bennett added.

"Fortune... I have heard it said, favors the bold, Leland. Are you indeed, bold?" Simone asked.

"In hindsight, perhaps not as often as I might have been. Where the future is concerned, we shall see."

The gathering eventually wound down with each guest thanking Bennett for the invitation, the meal, and the camaraderie. Russell and Inez had agreed beforehand not to leave together, continuing at least for the moment, some degree of privacy regarding their involvement. Delgado left in his military vehicle. Simone's driver, Mateo, had waited patiently outside for the get-together to conclude, so she offered Father Alonso a ride. He humbly accepted knowing this would give him an opportunity to discuss a situation better broached discretely.

"Simone. It has come to my attention that you will soon be adding to your staff."

"How diplomatic of you to say staff rather than stable. And just how did this come to your attention?"

"From both Elena Esperaza and her father."

"From both? But not at the same time, I wager."

"No. Not at the same time, and not from the same point of view."

"Well, I know what he thinks, what about her?"

"You have not spoken with her yet?"

"No."

"She does not want it. She is frightened. And she knows it is wrong."

"Most young girls are initially fearful about such things. They quickly get over it. Right and wrong are subjective, whether you will admit it or not."

"There must be others... who are perhaps more willing."

"There are always others. But I don't take on just anyone. Elena is young, beautiful, and I am told intelligent. Qualities not found everywhere."

"And it does not matter to you that she is against this?"

"One is often against what one does not know."

"She knows what will be expected of her."

"But she doesn't know that she will come to deal with it more readily than she imagines."

"I promised her I would do what I could and—"

"You have spoken to her father?"

"Yes. He was unyielding."

"And now you have spoken to me. Therefore you have done what you promised."

"But—"

"Father, I am not an ogre. Elena will not be mistreated or harmed in any way. She will simply be taught how to engage in behavior that virtually all women—with the exception I suppose of nuns—engage in around the world. I will personally take her under my wing. At first, she will merely be a house servant. Cooking, cleaning, serving drinks, food, that sort of thing. As she sees that my clients are not monsters, but simply men in need of compassion and tenderness, nature will take its course."

"It's not compassion and tenderness I'm concerned about. It's passion and lust."

"It's always been a mystery to me how celibate priests think they know what is best regarding sex in one's life."

"We know what Jesus said about it."

"Another celibate, as I recall."

"You should not blaspheme, Simone."

"And you should not meddle in my business, Father. For many years we have coexisted peacefully. Your church's religion and my house's recreation… sin on Saturday and salvation on Sunday. The people want both. I suggest we continue to give them what they want."

Chapter 17

Having circled back to spend some quality time with Inez after Bennett's dinner party, it was almost two in the morning before Russell returned to his cabin. He expected the coatimundi, Bolivar, to be waiting for him. He didn't expect the coati to be waiting on Elena's shoulder. She was slumped in the upholstered, but weather-beaten chair he had recently purchased from the secondhand store as his one sop to domesticity. Russell was hesitant to wake her up, but the lateness of the hour and her unexpected presence made him worry that something could be very wrong.

Russell put his hand on Elena's shoulder and gingerly shook her. She awoke and rubbed her eyes.

"Elena… are you all right? What are you doing here?"

"Your back door was unlocked."

"Yes? Have to pay more attention to that. But still, why are you here? And so late."

"I had no place else to go."

"Why did you have to go anywhere? Has something happened?"

"I've run away."

"Run away… from what, or who… I mean what's going on?"

"My father. He has made a deal with the woman who runs that place. He is forcing me to go there."

"What woman? What place are you talking about?"

"The woman they call Simone. And that house of hers."

It took a moment for Russell to make sense of what she was saying. Yet when he did, it seemed to make no sense to him.

"Simone? The woman who runs that… club? The one with the women?"

"The *putas*. My father is making me become one."

"Elena… no father would do that. There must be some mistake."

"There is no mistake. He says that our family needs the money. That it is my duty to help. But I do not want to. So I ran away."

"But it's the middle of the night. Your parents will be so worried."

"I waited until they were asleep. They won't know I am gone until they wake up in the morning."

It had already been a long night for Russell. He wasn't in a hurry to make it even longer. And the more he thought about it, the more he realized that there was little he could do in the dead of night.

"Well, look," he began, "you're tired, I'm tired, and your parents are still asleep. Let's try to get some rest and we'll look into this in the morning."

"So, I can stay?"

"For tonight, yes. I don't want you running around so late. There's a cot in the closet. I'll get it and sleep on that. You take the bed."

"Oh no. I cannot put you out of your bed. I will sleep in this chair."

"No. You'll wake up feeling terrible. I'll get the cot. It's no problem."

"You are so kind. *Gracias* for letting me stay here. *Muchos gracias.*"

Bolivar wanted to say thanks as well. With his tail pointing straight up, he leapt from the chair to Russell's shoulder.

"He is so funny. I love Bolivar," Elena said.

"Well, he apparently loves you, too. Of course, I haven't met anyone yet that he doesn't love. I'll get the cot."

*   *   *

Morning came sooner than Russell wanted it to, but a few days earlier he had spotted some overturned sand on the beach where eggs had been buried. He needed to make sure they were still undisturbed. So with eyes only half open, he willed himself to plod down the hill to check on them. Elena was still asleep. Russell assumed she was exhausted from the night before so he made a point not to wake her until he got back. With him at the beach and her under the covers, neither heard the sound of Inez's scooter as she pulled it off to the side of the road outside the cabin. For some reason unknown even to her, she had awakened far earlier than usual with a ravenous appetite and decided to pop in on Russell and take him to breakfast. Finding the front door locked, she walked around to the back to see if she could slip in and surprise him. Turning the knob and slipping in quietly, she did not find him, and the surprise was on her.

Inez stood staring, momentarily unable to grasp what she was seeing. There was this girl—this beautiful, very young girl—lying sound asleep in the middle of Russell's rumpled sheets. *What the hell?* That was her first thought. Her second thought was that Russell had left her bed the night before only to come back here and crawl into the sack with this child! Okay, perhaps 'child' was stretching it a bit, but certainly no more than a teenager. How could he do such a thing? Had she misjudged him completely? She realized she had no real claim on him, but still. This just seemed beyond the pale. Such was her shock and disappointment that she turned and hurried back outside without ever seeing the cot on the other side of the room. Straddling her scooter, she gunned what little engine there was and took off while wiping a tear from her eye.

Chapter 18

The telephone conversation had gotten past the initial pleasantries quickly. Now it was on to the business at hand.

"I understand that the former WCO employee is dead?"

"Yes. An unfortunate accident."

"That sort of thing is not good. It increases the profile of the property. Just the opposite of what we want."

"I understand, but who can account for accidents? They happen."

"You must understand that if my group is going to make this work we need to keep negative publicity... in fact, *any* and *all* publicity to a minimum."

"I understand completely."

"You also need to know that the price for inclusion has now gone up."

"But we had agreed upon a figure. I've already secured a commitment from my cohorts. I can't go back to them for more."

"Then you'll simply have to find additional investors. It shouldn't be that difficult. You know how lucrative this will be for those who get in on the ground floor. Not just initially. The ongoing return will be substantial as well."

"It was my intention to keep local participation to a minimum."

"Yes. Well, you know what they say about intentions and the road to hell. The officials we have to lobby are many, and they are costly. If you can't increase your own contribution, then you'll just have to find additional funds elsewhere... or withdraw."

"No. I don't want out. I'll see what I can do. Has return on investment been altered?"

"No. It's still based on contribution. Until all the seed money is acquired."

"All right. Might as well get on with it, then. How much more do I need to come up with?"

Chapter 19

When Russell returned from the beach, he woke Elena and they again discussed her plight. He still found it almost impossible to believe that her father would want her to do such a thing. But he realized that, as much as he tried, he could never really understand the depths of her family's poverty. She told him that she had spoken with Father Alonso and that he was trying to do whatever he could to change her father's mind. Elena was unaware that the priest had spoken to Simone as well and that both appeared unyielding.

Russell was concerned that Elena's absence would cause her family grave concern. He told her that he would speak with Father Alonso and see if the priest was making any headway with her father, but that she should return to her home right away and make up some excuse as to why she was gone to tell her family when they awoke.

Elena thanked him for trying to help, and then she agreed to return home. Russell had no way of knowing if she was serious about either.

When he arrived at the church, the doors were closed and Russell paused before ascending the stairs that fronted them.

It had been some time since he had even considered entering a house of worship. The discipline he had shown as a child in attending church with his mother had been replaced with an apathy toward religion as he grew older. The thought of venerating an omnipotent and all-forgiving deity had vanished completely in a night he was still unable to expunge from his memory. The thought of it even now kept his feet from moving forward. He stood in place, momentarily forgetting why he had come. Russell wondered for an instant if it was some sort of heavenly sign when the doors began to open. Then he realized it was simply Father Alonso coming outside.

"Oh, good day, Señor Russell. How nice to see you. Were you on your way in?"

"Well, yes and no, I guess. I really stopped by just to see you, if you have a moment."

"I always have a moment for people of our community. What can I do for you?"

"Actually, it's not about me. It's regarding a friend of mine. I think you know her… Elena Esperaza."

"Why certainly. I know Elena. A beautiful young soul. May I ask, how do you know Elena?"

"I met her on the hill above the nesting beach one day. She was watching for sea turtles."

"Yes, she is an animal lover, I believe. I can tell by the way she is so gentle and kind to her burro, Pepito."

"She seemed to be genuinely interested. So I've been showing her some of my responsibilities and giving her information about preservation and wildlife."

"I see. But how does this relate to me?"

Now that it was time to be specific, Russell hesitated momentarily, then continued.

"Father, Elena has confided in me. She told me… and she said that you know of this… that her father is planning to have her work at Simone's…"

"Place of business, shall we say? Yes. She has spoken to me of this."

"And she said you've talked to her father as well."

"I have."

"How can he do such a thing, Father Alonso? How can he even consider it?"

"From my standpoint as a priest, Mr. Russell, I can tell you there is no justification for his action. I am sure from your standpoint, as a moral if not a terribly religious man, you cannot justify it either. But as a man with multiple mouths to feed, a man whose family is so poor… I can at least understand what he *thinks* his justification is."

"But she's so young… and surely, innocent."

"Age, where this sort of thing is involved, can be very different in different parts of the world."

"I understand that. But, still, it's just not right. She says you're talking to him."

"I have talked to him. Unfortunately to no avail. I have also talked to Simone."

"Really? What was her response?"

"She is first and foremost a businesswoman. She thinks mostly of profit and loss. With Elena, she stands to profit substantially."

"But—"

"But she is also a woman. A woman not without an intimate past of her own. She is convinced that Elena will not be harmed physically, and that emotionally, the girl will get past the initial beginnings, and come to realize that what she does is not a reflection of who she is. Others formerly in her employ have gone on to lead what you and I might call normal lives."

"Yeah, well, some things are normal and some things aren't.

And this doesn't seem normal to me at all. And it certainly doesn't to Elena. This is something she absolutely doesn't want to do."

"Being able to do *only* what one wants is a very American luxury, I think. Retiro de Santos is not the USA."

"Someone else told me more or less the same thing not too long ago."

"We can only do what we can do. Sometimes that means letting go and putting the future in the hands of a higher authority."

"You mean God, I guess. Father, I haven't seen that work out well in the past."

"You are a young man. I am sure there is still much you haven't seen."

"I see how young Elena is. And I see that she hates what her father's making her do. So do I."

What was left of their conversation ended less than conclusively. Father Alonso said he'd continue to use whatever powers of persuasion he might have with Elena's father and Simone, but to Russell, he didn't sound like a man who thought he'd be successful. He indicated that Simone had told him the girl would initially be involved only with cooking and cleaning, not the roles of the other women in the house. That might at least buy more time to reverse Elena's fate. The American wasn't sure what to do next, but he wanted to share his indecision with someone. So he left to find Inez.

She had not answered when Russell called to tell her he was coming over. Her place in the village was only a short walk from the church but when he knocked on the door there was no response. Thinking she might be trying to talk tourists into having their caricatures done, he proceeded to the hotel. There were a few people having breakfast outdoors in the courtyard but no Inez. A stroll through the restaurant inside produced the same result. He was about to leave when he spotted her walking across the lobby with a small easel in her right hand and painting paraphernalia under her left arm. She reached the elevator just as he reached her.

"Inez, glad I caught you. Do you have a minute?"

"Can you push that button?"

He pushed it. "Guess you've got a commission, huh?"

The elevator doors opened.

"Can you hold this a second?" Inez asked, raising the easel in her hand.

He took it from her.

"Maybe after—"

With her free hand, she delivered a roundhouse right to his jaw. The resulting smack turned heads in the lobby.

As the American staggered backward, Inez pulled the easel from his hand and stepped into the elevator. She then leaned it against the side wall so she could push the button for her floor and calmly present Russell with her middle finger as the doors closed.

Chapter 20

Simone's domicile was a home in more ways than one. In addition to being where she lived, it also was her place of business, as well as a residence hotel for the women who worked there. The three-story Victorian structure was painted bright purple with white trim and was located close enough to the village center to make it easily accessible, yet far enough away to provide some measure of privacy. The house sat on a plot of land at the end of a dirt road continually fortified with rock and gravel. Those who went down that road would find no other houses, buildings, or destinations of any sort. Of course, those who went down that road had only one destination in mind.

The first floor consisted of a porch that ran around three sides of the home. Just inside the front door was a narrow entryway that when traversed, led to a huge drawing room filled with settees, love seats, sofas, and chairs—all upholstered and overstuffed for maximum comfort. A wet bar was wedged into one corner of the room, and even though sconces were strategically placed on each of the walls, an immense chandelier hung from the ceiling. It was adorned with hundreds of individual mirrored-glass rectangles that shimmered like sunlight on water. The room had been wired for sound and unobtrusive speakers enabled Bach, Beethoven, and more to entertain decorously. Simone felt that classical music set the appropriate tone for how she expected both her guests and her employees to behave—at least while they were in the drawing room.

The remainder of the ground floor consisted of a dining room sufficiently-sized to seat eight or more, though large parties were not common. Two bathrooms were just off the drawing room. In the rear, an oversized kitchen ran the length of the house and connected with a laundry room whose continuing functionality was vital to the operation's ongoing success. They went through a lot of sheets.

The second floor contained a large bathroom designed to accommodate multiple individuals. The rest of the floor consisted of the women's rooms. This was where services were provided during business hours and privacy was allowed when everyone was off the clock.

While a maid was employed for ongoing cleaning, each staff member was required to keep her area neat and tidy. The last thing any of the women wanted was for a customer to complain to Simone about the surroundings in which business was conducted. The madam could be more than stern.

The third floor was Simone's living quarters. Her office and bedroom were both fitted with French doors that opened onto balconies. Her private bath was both large and luxurious. Rank has its privileges.

Behind the home, the backyard had been turned into a flower garden that sprinkled the area with color. Hibiscus, marigolds, poinsettias, dahlias, and more lent their beauty to the foliage surrounding a small cast iron table and chairs often used for coffee and contemplation. The furniture was occupied this day by Simone and her guest, Leland Bennett, who had asked if he could come over and discuss something that might be beneficial to both of them. She had readily granted his request.

"Simone, what I'm going to share with you is of a highly confidential nature."

"Leland, do you know anyone who is more discreet than I am? More often than not my business depends on it."

"You recall at dinner the other night, how the talk turned into a bit of a philosophical discussion about helping and protecting people versus animals, or wildlife?"

"I recall."

"Well, the question has become a lot less philosophical and a lot more practical."

"There's no need to be cagey, Leland. Simply get to the point."

"All right. For some time now, I have been involved with a consortium that is considering a huge investment here in Retiro de Santos."

"What sort of investment?"

"A land acquisition. One that would be quite expensive."

"Is your property involved?"

"Not exactly."

"And what *exactly* does not exactly mean?"

"Well, they're not interested in my property, but they are interested in my participation."

"Your participation? I take that to mean your money."

"Yes. A great deal of money actually. While I'm prepared to supply a large part of it, I'm simply not able to raise the entire amount on my own."

"So you come to me."

"I thought, as one our community's most insightful business owners, you'd be able to see the opportunity that exists?"

"Leland, please put the compliments on hold and get to the point. What is all this about?"

"It's about the beach that is currently off-limits to people but not sea turtles."

"The beach under the control of the WCO?"

"Yes."

"The beach overseen by young Mr. Russell?"

"Yes."

"But what makes this... what did you call it?"

"A consortium?"

"Yes. What makes this consortium think they can acquire it?"

"They have extremely close contacts with those in high levels of government. Even into the governor's office itself. Contacts that they constantly remind me are quite costly."

"And if they were successful in acquiring the beach, just what do they plan to do with it?"

"They plan to build, Simone. Hotels. Condos. Timeshares. Restaurants and clubs. 'Multiple-use property' is how they refer to it. Multiple uses that mean jobs for the people of Retiro de Santos."

"Spare me the chamber of commerce pitch, Leland. Just tell me what's in it for you... and perhaps me if I'm able... or willing... to help."

"Return on investment, Simone. For those who come in on the ground floor, and help provide the seed capital, a percentage of profits is guaranteed for the development of all properties on the site. With potential participation in actual operational profits as well."

"And why are they reaching out to you? Surely they have other resources they can go to for money?"

"Local participation is particularly important. They need to show their government contacts that there is community support for this kind of undertaking. From a public relations point of view, it is vital."

Simone, never one to let an opportunity slip by, kept her questions relevant.

"Would it be just you and I supplying the local support?"

"No. I won't have the wherewithal to meet their requirement even with your participation. There are others I can approach, but I'd like to keep that confidential for now, just as I'll withhold any input regarding your involvement."

"If I get involved."

"Yes. If. But if you do, I can tell you of one other who is already on board."

"And who would that be?"

"Delgado."

"He has financial resources?"

"Some. But it was important that he be for this project rather than against it. Considering he's the closest thing to local government that Retiro de Santos has, it will be seen as a plus by the authorities who will eventually be contacted. Needless to say, he was extremely enthusiastic. The prospect of a big return on a small investment is something he is really looking forward to."

"I can see where he would have a way to come up with additional funds. He puts the bite on other businesses like he does on ours."

"Yes. Protection is an old racket, but a profitable one."

Simone added. "He's not altogether stable, you know. His calm demeanor hides a violent temper. Don't ask me how I know."

"He'll be more of an asset than a problem. As I said, we need him."

"You're already saying *we*."

"I don't mean to take you for granted."

"No. You just mean to take me. But I'm inclined to let you. Just how much do you need?"

Chapter 21

Russell had no idea that Inez had discovered Elena in his bed and jumped to the wrong conclusion. He was therefore mystified as to why she had socked him and given him the one-finger salute. *I think I'll just wait for her,* he said to himself, realizing that something was definitely amiss. An hour later, he was still occupying a chair in the lobby and trying to come up with what he might have done to provoke her right cross. Russell was so engrossed in his mental deliberations that he failed to notice the attractive young woman who entered the lobby and went to the registration counter to check-in. When she gave her name, Anne Morrow, to the clerk, something started to invade Russell's thought processes. Something from out of the past. *Anne? Anne Morrow?* It can't be. But it was.

Russell sprang from his chair, crossed the lobby, and headed toward her. She was vaguely aware of someone approaching, then all of a sudden she took a look at the man coming her way.

"Russell?"

"Anne! What are you doing here?"

"I've come to see you. I couldn't help myself."

Before it happened, before the night everything came apart for Stephen Russell, he and Anne were an item. More than an item, really. There had been some talk about marriage, or at least the possibility of it. She was a graduate student who had caught his eye one day on campus as she came out of the auditorium and strode across the quad on her way to the student union. Lithe of frame and long of limb, she carried herself like the athlete she was. Years of swimming had kept her in peak condition and imbued her with confidence that came out in the way she carried herself. Her long auburn ponytail bounced as she walked. She held her head high. Her emerald eyes focused on where she was going while Russell's focused on her. He was immediately smitten. Enough so that he trailed along behind her, followed her into the building, saw the coffee and Danish she was ordering, and asked for the same. Fortunately, the room was full enough that he could credibly say, "Wow, it's really crowded in here. Would you mind if I shared your table? Looks like we're having the same thing." She looked around, accepted his explanation, and asked him to sit. Introductions were swapped and over the course of the next half hour, their conversation led to an exchange of email addresses, which led to a first date, which led to a lot more time together both on campus and off, which led to the two becoming lovers and talking about a potential future together. But that was all before the night it happened.

"Did you somehow learn I was coming?" she asked. "Is that why you're at the hotel?"

"No. I had no idea. I just happened to be here this morning. But I can't believe you're here. I wish you would have let me know in advance."

"I thought you'd try to talk me out of it."

"I would have."

"That's why I didn't do it."

"But how did you know... I mean... who told—"

"Your parents. I asked how you were doing. They told me you had taken a position with The World Conservation Organization and where you'd been sent. They didn't know of my plans. They assumed I was just curious."

"Well, what are your plans?"

"Plan, singular. I really don't have more than one. I just wanted to see you, and talk... and maybe see if there was anything left of what we once shared."

"I just wish you would have let me know. I mean, there's a lot going on right now and..."

"I'm not going to get in your way, Stephen. I just want us to have the talk we never had. You left so suddenly. And stayed away so long."

"Anne, you know why—"

"I know why," she interrupted, "but I don't know how you came to the decision you did. And I don't know what that means for the future. The future together we often talked about. I thought I had come to grips with not really knowing. But I knew I wouldn't be able to let it go until I knew you wanted me to. Funny, isn't it? I was always the one with a purpose in mind, a goal to achieve. Now my goal is to simply know for sure whether there's any hope for *us* anymore. One way or the other. So I can get on with my life, you know."

"Yes. I do know. That's one thing about you that hasn't changed. Your dislike of ambiguity. Your need for certainty. Must have been all those swimming competitions. A definitive time at the end of the race."

"That's right, Stephen. You win or you lose. But at least you know where the hell you are."

He was momentarily unable to replay.

"Look. We're certainly not going to hash all this out in the lobby. I've got my key."

"Sure. Let me help you with your bag. Looks too heavy for you but I know you'd never admit it."

They walked to the elevator and stood together, waiting for the doors to open. When they did, they were face-to-face with Inez.

Once again, Russell was momentarily speechless. Inez wasn't. She cracked sarcastically, "Well, at least this one's an adult." Then, on her way past them, she made a point of stepping on Russell's foot. Hard.

Chapter 22

The day had fulfilled its promise with the sun warming everything beneath it. Now the moon had risen and its light shone on a lone figure walking toward the police station. Reaching the door, the figure hesitated for a moment, removed his straw hat, then turned the handle and went inside.

There was no officer at the reception desk. The comandante had let Garza leave. Things were slow even for Retiro de Santos. The door to Delgado's office was open, enabling him to see the man that entered and now simply stood with hat in hand, looking around.

"*Hombre. Aquí,*" Delgado said loudly.

The man acknowledged he had heard by nodding his head. He then walked over slowly and the two men conversed in Spanish.

"Who are you? And what do you need?" Delgado asked.

"I am Miguel Esperaza. My daughter, Elena, is missing."

"What do you mean, missing? For how long?"

"She was not here when I awoke this morning. My wife said she has not been home all day. It is now dark. Still, she does not come home. I fear something has happened."

"How old is your daughter?"

"Sixteen."

"Perhaps she is with her school friends… or out with some boy."

"I asked at the home of her friends. They have not seen her. And there is no boy."

"Fathers are often the last to know."

"I know there is no boy. My wife tells me she has no sweetheart."

"Was there trouble in your house? Do you think she ran away? Why would she do something like that?"

"There was no trouble. Disagreements, yes. But no trouble. She always does what I tell her… eventually."

"Then… eventually… she will likely return."

"I am afraid something has happened. You are the police. You are supposed to help."

Delgado sighed and bemoaned the fact that he had let his underling go home. Best to get on with it he thought, or they'd be there all night. He looked in his desk and found the form that he needed.

"Can you read and write?"

"*No, señor.*"

"*Comandante.*" Delgado corrected him.

"*No, Comandante.*"

It's going to be a long night, Delgado thought but soldiered on. "All right. You talk, I'll write. What does your daughter look like?"

Chapter 23

The key to a long conversation is the beginning. Does it start with excuses, regrets, and recriminations? If it does, it will likely die a premature death. If it begins differently, however, with curiosity, inquiries, and remembrances, then it will likely meet or exceed its expected lifespan. Russell and Anne's conversation, aided first by a bottle of wine, then followed later by another, lasted beyond the light of day and deep into the cloak of night. Places they had been, things they had done, people they had known—all were side streets they were able to wander down before taking the boulevard to where both knew they had to go eventually. Once they arrived, there was no turning back.

"It wasn't your fault, you know?"

"Everyone says that, Anne. I know better."

"No one blames you. No one ever has."

"It's not about what others think. It never has been."

"You never saw a therapist, did you?"

"That kind of thing isn't for me."

"Can't you see what one would say now, after the choice you made, and coming here?"

"Actually I can. I'm sure some convincingly empathetic shrink would say I've chosen to hide from everything and everyone connected to that night, and that I'm trying to somehow atone, or do penance for what I think I'm guilty of."

"Well, if you understand that…?"

"I understand that he'd be right, but what he'd be wrong about is whether or not I should be doing it. He'd say I shouldn't. I know I have to. He'd say I'm just trying to do something good to make up for something bad. I'd say what the hell's wrong with that? He'd say you can't change the past. I'd say, how brilliantly profound."

"I don't think that's what you'd say, Stephen."

"Oh no, what would I say?"

"Knowing you, if he said you can't change the past, you'd probably say… no shit."

Russell couldn't help but smile.

It was extremely late when both decided they had more or less talked and drank themselves into both physical and emotional fatigue. Anne suggested Russell should simply spend the night there. He was too tired to argue and prepared to stretch out on the couch. She told him not to be silly and come to bed. He did. But during the silent journey from full moon to bright sun, all they shared was sleep.

When they awoke in the morning, both thought of the other less as a former lover, and more as an old friend. They somehow knew that just as you can't change the past, you can't recreate it either. And each was at peace with that.

"Would you like to see my beach?" Russell asked.

"No. I don't think so, Stephen. I think the sooner we get on with whatever lies ahead for both of us, the better off we'll be. I'll just gather my things and head back to the mainland. I can catch a flight this evening."

"But you've come so far."

"Yes. And you haven't," she replied, with no trace of venom or ill will. "We are who we are, Stephen. Not who we were. I know that now."

"I'm glad you came. I guess we needed a real ending, didn't we?"

"I did. And I want you to know that what we had before was wonderful. I don't regret a minute of it. But I don't plan to spend another moment reliving it. Time to get on with life. That's what I plan to do. Hope you will, too."

"You're a wonderful person, Anne. You deserve to be happy."

"So do you, Stephen. I hope you realize that."

Chapter 24

When Russell returned to his cabin he got a double dose of surprise. The first was that the place was immaculate. Bed made. Floor swept. Table tops dusted. Dishes washed and put away. The second surprise was that Elena was still sitting in the chair he had found her in the night before last. Though this time, Bolivar wasn't on her shoulder. He had gone to get his breakfast.

"Elena."

"*Hola*, Stephen."

"You didn't have to clean up. How long have you been back here?"

"Well, you see… I never left."

"What? You didn't go home. You haven't been back to see your parents? They're going to be worried sick."

"I do not think so. If they really cared about me, my father would not want me to work at Simone's."

"Any parent would be worried to death if a child didn't come home not just one night, but two."

"I am not a child. There are some girls my age who are already married here in Retiro de Santos."

"Believe me, to your parents… at least to your mother anyway, you are a child and I'm sure both of them will be worried."

Elena rose from the chair and began to walk around as she talked. "Stephen, I think I have found a way to solve this problem with my father."

That seemed to come out of nowhere, Russell thought. "Really? You think there's a solution?"

"Yes."

"Well, tell me. What is it?"

"We can get married. Then I will be your wife. And father will have one less mouth to feed."

Russell made a point of not laughing or calling her solution ridiculous. He simply said straightforwardly, "No, Elena. We can't get married."

"But I would make a very good wife. Look how well I have cleaned your house. I can cook, too. If you had anything to cook."

"It's impossible, Elena. You're too young to get married."

"If I'm old enough to work at Simone's, then I'm old enough to get married."

Hard to argue that point, Russell thought, *better to simply be firm*. "Elena, we are not going to get married."

The corners of her mouth turned down as she said, "Am I not desirable enough?"

"No. It's not that. You're a lovely girl."

She walked toward him as she said, "I am not experienced in making a man happy in bed, but you could teach me. I learn very fast."

Without even realizing it, he held his hand out as if to stop her. "Elena. Please. I just don't think of you in that way. You're too young for me to think of you as a potential wife."

"Is there someone else?" She asked.

In her question, Russell recognized the opportunity to reject her idea without completely rejecting her. "Ah… yes, as a matter of fact, there is. I'm seeing someone."

"Someone," she asked tentatively, "you are in love with?"

Oh, God, what do I say to that, Russell asked himself. But he didn't have to answer. Just then there was a knock on the door.

Russell paused for a moment, not sure whether to go to the door and not sure what to do with Elena. The knock came again. This time followed by a voice.

"Señor Russell? Are you there? This is Comandante Delgado."

Quickly, Russell held one finger in front of his mouth, urging Elena to keep quiet. Then he took her by the arm and walked her to the closet. Again he motioned for her to be silent as he moved her inside and shut the door.

"One second, Comandante. Be right there," he yelled. Then pausing for another few seconds, he went to the door and opened it.

"Sorry, Comandante, I was in the toilet."

"I hope I did not rush you?"

"Oh no," Russell said, forcing a smile. "I was finished."

"Would you mind if we talked inside?"

"Ah… of course not. Please, come in."

They walked inside and Delgado took a look around the cabin.

"I must say, Señor Russell, you keep a very tidy place. One does not always see that in the home of a bachelor."

"Yes, well, I just like to keep things ship-shape, you know. Always have. Not really sure why. So, what can I do for you?"

"I wanted to let you know that we currently have a missing person's case we are looking into."

"Really?"

"Yes. A young girl."

"I see. But why would you contact me about this?"

"It is not personal. We are canvassing the area. Letting everyone know."

"Oh, of course. How long has the girl been missing?"

"Two days now. Her parents are very concerned."

"Well, I can certainly understand that."

Suddenly, Bolivar returned from his breakfast mission through the back window. The coati leapt from the table in the kitchen to the middle of the room where the two men were standing.

"Oh, that's just Bolivar," Russell said. "Pay him no mind, he thinks he runs the place."

"Yes. There are some who regard these animals as pets. Frankly, I find them a nuisance, best used for target practice."

Eager to get rid of the policeman, Russell would have let Delgado's comment go, obnoxious as it was, but then Bolivar scampered across the floor and over to the closet door, where he began to scratch it with his front claws.

"Perhaps there is something in there he wants," the policeman said.

"Oh, no," Russell replied, as he hurried across the room, opened the closet door just a crack so the coati could dash in, then quickly closed it. "He simply likes dark places. Cave-like, I guess."

"Getting back to the subject at hand," Delgado began. "The missing girl's name is Elena Esperaza."

Russell wasn't sure whether to react or not. Delgado forced a decision.

"I assume you don't know her."

Did he really assume that, Russell wondered? *Or, had he talked to someone, say Father Alonso perhaps, who might have mentioned their discussion of Elena?* Russell opted for the truth.

At least part of the truth. "Elena. Yes, I do know her."

"You do."

"Yes. She showed an interest in the sea turtles once, and from time to time I've shown her more of their habitat and given her information about them."

"How interesting. Do you have any idea where she might be? Has she ever confided in you about friends or anyone she might have gone to see?"

Time for truth was over, Russell decided. At least for the time being. "No... she's never really talked about herself or her friends. Our conversations were always about the turtles."

"Well, as I said, I'm sure you can appreciate her parents' concern. The quicker we find her, the sooner we can put her loved ones at ease. If you see or hear from her, you will let me know immediately, yes?"

"Why, yes. Of course. But I doubt she'll contact me."

"I doubt it as well. But should she..."

"I'll be sure to let you know."

"*Muchas gracias*," Delgado said. "I will be going now. I have others to contact."

"Thank you for letting me know, Comandante. Good luck with your search."

When Elena heard Russell tell the policeman goodbye and then close the front door, she stepped out of the closet. The look on her face told the American she was a lot more fearful now than before. So was he.

Chapter 25

The veranda at Leland Bennett's home offered a stunning view of the sea. So upon the arrival of his guest, he suggested they move outside to share the beautiful day with a dry white wine to accompany their conversation. Bennett had initially called her to ask if she had a few minutes she could spend with him, as well as offering to meet at her flat or wherever she liked in the village. She had suggested his place, saying that she wanted to get away from town for a while anyway.

"So, is the wine satisfactory, or would you like to try something else?"

"Leland, it's delightful. As is this gorgeous view," Inez answered. "It's always a treat to come to your place."

"And you always brighten this old relic up, my dear. I'm speaking of both the house and myself."

"You're not old, Leland. And neither you nor this house are relics. You're both mature and distinguished. Qualities that are seriously lacking in some people I know."

"Is that why you wanted to get away from town for a bit? Someone being difficult about your work?"

"No. Not work. But you didn't call to hear my troubles.

You had something you wanted to discuss."

"I did and I do. But it's a lovely day. Neither of us is in a hurry. I'd be remiss if I didn't try to help with whatever seems to be troubling you."

"It's nothing, really."

"If it were nothing, you wouldn't have felt the need to get away. Come now, ladies first, as they say."

"I don't confide in many people, you know. I've always been a bit of a loner."

"Then I would be even more honored if you have something you'd like to discuss."

"This would stay just between you and me, right?"

"Absolutely, Inez. As far as I'm concerned, private conversations are sacrosanct."

"Okay, then. Maybe it will help to get it off my chest."

"I'm an excellent listener."

"You may, or may not know, that Stephen Russell and I have been seeing each other."

"While I didn't know for sure, I must admit to being intrigued by a few furtive glances I saw pass between you two the other night at dinner."

"Really? And I thought we were being so sly."

"It's difficult to hide mutual attraction. And I assume it is mutual."

"Well, it is... or it was... or... oh hell, when I say we've been seeing each other, what I really mean is—"

"As you said earlier, Inez, I'm both mature and sophisticated. I know what seeing each other *really* means."

"Well... we've been seeing each other pretty damn hot and heavy."

"You're both young, healthy, attractive, and unattached... I'm not surprised."

"The surprise was all mine, believe me. I just recently saw the jerk going up in the hotel elevator with some blond bimbo. He looked guilty as hell."

"It might have been an acquaintance or a relative."

"Had it been either one of those, he would have introduced me, right?"

"Well, if he saw you, I suppose."

"Oh, he saw me all right. I made sure of that. And no introduction. Not even an acknowledgment. But that's not the worst of it."

"There's more?"

"I'll say there's more. I happened to go out to his place early the other morning. I go in the front door, and what do I see? A girl in his bed! It was obvious she spent the night there. And when I say a girl, I mean a girl. She had to be a teenager. And not a very old one at that."

"Really? Russell never struck me as some unbridled Lothario."

"Looks can be deceiving, Leland. I thought he was a good guy, too. Now... I mean here he is boffing me, and at the same time he's having it off with some mainland blonde plus a kid half his age. The bastard!"

"Have you confronted him about this behavior?"

"Yes and no. I socked him in the jaw and ground my heel into his arch, but I haven't actually spoken to him."

Bennett paused before responding, giving himself a moment to picture Inez's vivid description. "Well, you know it is possible that there is some explanation, which—"

"Come on Leland," Inez interrupted. "If it walks like a duck..."

"Yes. I understand what you're saying. But, getting back to the young woman that you saw in his bed. Do you think she's a local?"

"Yes. I met her at his place once before and he told me they were just friends. But if that isn't robbing the cradle, I don't know what is."

"Inez, you must have some feelings for Russell, or you wouldn't be so irate. I think you should have a conversation with him… without fisticuffs… so you'll know for certain. You're an insightful woman. Listen to what he has to say. You'll be able to tell if he's telling the truth, lying, or just trying to string you along."

Her shoulders sagged as she released a sigh and said, "Oh, God. I guess you're right. I probably should at least listen to what he has to say. But if it's an obvious whopper, then a knee to the groin might be just what's called for. Perhaps I should have another glass of that wine."

"Splendid idea," Bennett said, as he rose, picked up the bottle, and poured another for Inez and himself. "Getting it off your chest, plus this superb Puligny Montrachet, should make you feel infinitely better."

Taking a sip, she said, "It is excellent, and I do feel better. But enough about my love life, or the burning embers of it. Let's move on to what you called me about. What was on *your* mind?"

Chapter 26

Garza, in the outer office, put the caller on hold. Then, because he had yet to master switching a call from one line to another, simply called out to his superior.

"Comandante, call for you on line one."

"Who is calling?"

"I forgot to ask."

"*Estúpido*," Delgado said under his breath. Then picked up the receiver and punched in.

"This is Comandante Delgado. Who is calling, please?"

"It's me," Bennett said. "Things are beginning to break our way."

"How so?"

"You advised me earlier that you were looking for a missing girl?"

"We still are."

"I have a lead for you."

"What is it?"

"Check the cabin of Stephen Russell."

"I was already at Russell's. He doesn't seem to know anything about the girl."

"Go back again. But this time use some degree of stealth, all right?"

"What makes you think the girl may be there?"

"I have it on good authority."

"From whom?"

"That is unimportant. What is important is that we have a chance to paint two pictures here."

"And those pictures are?"

"One is a picture of you. By finding the girl you've been looking for, you appear a civic hero. The other is Russell, who can be painted to appear a kidnapper, or worse."

"What could be worse than a kidnapper?"

"A defiler of young girls, perhaps."

"Where do you get such information?"

"Don't ask me that again. Just find out if he has a young girl in his cabin. And if he does, arrest him."

"But what if it's not the girl we're looking for?"

"Doesn't matter. You can still charge him with illegal relations with a minor."

"That may be a hard charge to prove... depending on what the minor says."

"It doesn't matter whether it is provable or not. It doesn't even matter if he winds up getting off later. What matters is that an employee of the World Conservation Organization will be seen as a probable pervert. Someone who preys on young women. That, along with the recent death of Thackery, will combine to paint the WCO in Retiro de Santos as particularly suspect. Key officials will see the organization in a highly negative light. And that can be very positive for us as the consortium lobbies those officials to retract their lease and approve our project."

"I see what you mean. As you said, things may indeed be breaking our way."

"Yes, but only if you find the girl... or a girl... with Russell in his place."

"A deputy and I will go there now," Delgado responded.

"Don't foul this up, Comandante. And take a camera with you," Bennett added. "You know what they say a good picture is worth."

Chapter 27

The sun was going down on the third day of Elena's disappearance. Since Delgado's earlier visit to Russell's cabin, the American and the young girl had been debating what to do. Elena was no longer pushing her marriage scheme. It had been an adolescent shot in the dark anyway. She wasn't in love with Russell, it just seemed preferable to the alternative looming on her horizon.

Occasionally sipping from a cup of coffee, Russell told her that he had talked to Father Alonso about her plight, but that the priest had no concrete solution to the problem. The more they talked, the more Russell could see that Elena's fear was not only rising, but also being compounded by severe depression that there was nothing anyone could do to alter her fate.

"Elena, even if you have to go there initially, Father Alonzo told me that Simone said you'd only be involved in household chores for a while."

"How long is *for a while*?" Elena asked. "You do not know. Neither do I."

"What I do know, is that we have to get you back home. The fact that the police are looking for you raises the stakes."

"Stakes? I do not understand."

"Sorry. What I meant is that everything is a lot more serious now. People are spending time, effort, and money looking for you. You don't want to get in trouble for pulling a hoax... playing a trick on everyone. The best thing to do is just be honest, especially with the police."

"That policeman who came... when I was hiding in the closet. I have heard his voice before. I am not sure where. But it was not that long ago."

"Yes, hiding you from him is one of the things we'll have to explain, I guess. But better to do that than try to put together a trail of lies. There's an old saying... *'Oh what a tangled web we weave when first we practice to deceive.'* It's from the Scottish author Sir Walter Scott. He wrote it over 200 years ago."

Slipping momentarily into wistfulness, Russell asked, "Did I ever tell you I was going to be a teacher?"

"Before your work with the turtles?"

"Yes. Before that."

"Why did you not become a teacher in your country? Why did you come here?"

Before Russell could decide how to dance around Elena's question, his front door was knocked off its hinges. The force sent it crashing to the floor. The shock brought a scream from Elena, and Russell spilled his coffee. The overweight Garza, in uniform, stepped through the now open doorway. He was holding a shotgun.

"¡*No te muevas!*" the portly policeman shouted.

"He said, don't move," Delgado, who had just come through the unlocked back door translated. Then added, "That was for your benefit, Señor Russell. I'm sure she understood."

Turning his gaze to the frightened girl, Delgado asked, "*Eres Elena Esperaza?*"

"*Sí*," was all her fear allowed her to say.

"Please rise, Señor Russell. We will all be going to the police station now."

"Comandante, let me explain. It's really all a misunder—"

"Later, *señor*. There will be time to explain things at my place, not yours."

Russell didn't argue. He didn't want to appear to be afraid, annoyed, or antagonistic. He felt the best thing to do was to simply follow Delgado's instructions. But he was concerned about Elena, who kept looking at the Comandante and appeared to be trembling with terror.

Russell tried to comfort her. "It's going to be okay," he said.

But the look on Elena's face made it obvious she didn't believe him.

Chapter 28

The ride to the police station was made in silence. Russell didn't want to provoke Delgado, and Elena was simply too scared to speak. Upon arrival, the comandante told Garza to take the girl to the small room they used for interrogations and private meetings. He then walked Russell over to a holding cell.

Delgado took him by the arm, opened the door, and guided him in.

"Comandante, please. Is this really necessary?"

"It is I believe referred to in your country as standard operating procedure."

There was an audible clank as the door of the cell closed and locked.

"But there's no need to put me in here. I've done nothing wrong."

"Nothing wrong, Señor Russell? What a curious thing to say."

"But if you'd just let me explain—"

Delgado interrupted, "Why don't I explain the situation to you? In Retiro de Santos, just as in other parts of the world, kidnapping is a crime."

"Kidnapping? What are you talking about?"

"I'm talking about holding an individual against her will."

"Look, it wasn't against her will, just ask Elena, she'll tell you."

"The young woman is obviously distraught. You may have brainwashed her as well."

Russell couldn't believe his ears. "Brainwashed? That's absurd."

"No, it is not absurd, *señor*. I believe it is referred to as Stockholm Syndrome. When the victim begins to identify and show feelings for her captor."

"Look, this is no Patty Hearst situation," Russell responded, stifling a chuckle and the thought that this was becoming almost comical.

"It can be a form of insanity," Delgado responded, "this I have read."

"Why are we even talking about kidnapping? That's not applicable here."

"That will be determined later."

"If you just let me—"

Delgado cut him off again. "To use your own word, what is also *applicable*, is the crime of sexual congress with a minor."

All of a sudden, Russell didn't see his situation as the least bit funny. "Hey. Now, wait a minute. Nothing like that went on. Ask her. Just ask her. She'll tell you. Nothing… nothing of that nature happened."

"Of course, I would expect you to deny such a transgression, but you have already proven yourself to be a liar."

"Liar? What are you talking about?"

"The other day, when I came to your cabin to inform you of our search, you said you knew nothing of her whereabouts. That was a lie. Was it not? It was also a crime as well… impeding an officer of the law in the performance of his duty."

Russell was momentarily mute. *Damn*, he thought to himself.

Why did I do that? What have I gotten myself into?

"Silent? I can understand why."

"Look, Comandante, this whole thing is a lot more complicated than you think. Why don't you just let me tell you exactly what's happened, then you can check with Elena. I'm sure she'll confirm what I say. This is all just a big mistake. You know me. We've socialized together. Had dinner at Bennett's the other night. Do I strike you as the kind of person who would do the sort of things you're accusing me of?"

"How you strike me is not relevant, *señor.* We will sort out what you are, or what you are not, in due course. But first, we must reunite a young girl with her family. That is what is most important. For now, you will remain here."

Delgado turned and began walking away. Russell stood there, hands on the bars that surrounded him. This was all crazy, he thought, and just as crazy was the fact that try as he might, he couldn't shake a phrase that kept running through his mind. A phrase from an old movie he had seen countless times as a child, "*Toto, we're not in Kansas anymore.*"

Chapter 29

Frightened as she was, had Elena been asked about Russell's involvement, she would have told the truth. But no one asked. She was kept alone in the small room until Delgado was ready to take her home to her father. It took a while for him to be ready because he first wanted to give an interview to the freelance stringer that passed as a local journalist. While there was only a weekly paper in Retiro de Santos, the policeman knew that the story would be sent to other outlets on the mainland. Delgado made a point of highlighting the charges that would be brought against Russell and ended the interview abruptly. He had no intention of letting the stringer talk to the accused or the girl in question. Plus, he knew there would be no immediate follow-up as the fellow, flippantly referred to as a reporter, was totally devoid of curiosity or ambition. As Bennett had suggested, the key was to get notoriety for the accusations. What happened after that was of little consequence.

Later, when Delgado drove Elena to her home, she cowered in the back of his vehicle, saying nothing. Unaware Russell had been jailed, she was also harboring a secret that terrified her. A terror that was only temporarily alleviated when the policeman left her with her family and departed.

*   *   *

A day and a half later, Russell was still incarcerated. He kept asking if Elena had cleared things up and Delgado kept telling him that the girl was still too frightened to talk about what happened to her. Russell didn't believe that, but there was nothing he could do. Judicial reform and anything resembling the rights of the accused were not part and parcel of legal practices in Retiro de Santos. However, at midday, Garza approached his cell with key in hand. After unlocking the door, he said to Russell, "*Se puede ir.*"

"I can go?" Russell hoped he was translating correctly as he used a hand gesture to denote leaving.

Garza didn't speak, but he did return the gesture. Russell wasted no time in exiting the cell. When he reached the building's foyer he saw Leland Bennett standing there.

"Leland?"

"Stephen, good to see you, lad."

"Leland, are you aware… did you know—"

"Yes. Know all about it. In fact, I'm one of the reasons you're free now."

"You are? Please tell me what's going on. They wouldn't tell me anything in there."

"Well, it appears that they've spoken with the girl and she confirmed that you neither kidnapped her nor harmed her in any way."

"I told them that when they first brought me here. What's taken so long?"

"Stephen, you should know by now that everything moves

at a snail's pace in Retiro de Santos. Especially the law."

"But what are you doing here? How did you learn of—"

"The only thing here that doesn't move at the speed of one of your turtles is rumor and gossip. I got word yesterday, but it was only today that I was able to convince Delgado to release you on your own recognizance."

"But you said Elena confirmed everything."

"She confirmed that you're not a kidnapper or a child molester. There's still that little matter of not being straightforward with Delgado when he originally went to your place. He's not totally convinced to let that go yet. But, as I said, he did allow you to be released for now… assuming I'd vouch for you."

"Thanks, Leland. I appreciate you standing up for me. But I find it laughable they can even bring up a potential sex crime with what Elena's father has planned for her."

"I'm not sure I know what you're referring to, but you have to remember that things are different here. Particularly as it relates to age of consent, parental rights, those sorts of things."

"I accept that things are different. I don't agree that they're right."

"That's certainly your prerogative, my boy. Listen, my car is here, why don't I give you a lift back to your place and you can tell me all about the plans you said that father has for his daughter. Not that we can do anything about it."

Chapter 30

Elena walked two steps behind her father as they slowly made their way to the big purple house down the dirt and gravel road. He carried a pillowcase over his shoulder with Elena's clothing. On her shoulders, she carried the weight of the world. She had not told her father, or anyone else, why she was in such fear of Comandante Delgado. It was obvious that her father felt subservient and in gratitude to him as well for finding and bringing his daughter home. It was hard for her to understand how the same heart could have room for those feelings yet be unable to grasp his own daughter's concerns. Maybe it was being an adult, she pondered. Maybe as one grows older one becomes immune to the feelings of others. Perhaps she would, too. She hoped not, but she was beginning to think it might be inevitable.

Almost an hour after they had begun their hike, they were within sight of their destination. On the second-floor, Mateo, a 230-pound block of muscle who also served as Simone's driver, handyman, bouncer, and occasional bed partner, was replacing a light on the balcony. When he saw the two approaching, he immediately stopped what he was doing and reported their upcoming arrival to his mistress.

Before Elena's father could use the ornamental knocker in the shape of a boar's head, Simone opened the front door. She greeted them warmly and with a smile. Years of practice had whittled away the insincerity, making it appear almost genuine.

"*Hola*, Mr. Esperaza. And this must be Elena. What a beautiful young woman you are."

She did not respond, but her father did. "The arrangement we agreed to?"

A lace-embroidered shawl was draped over Simone's shoulders and wrapped around her waist. She reached inside it, pulled out an envelope, and handed it to Elena's father.

"As we agreed," she said.

He took the envelope and secured it within his own waistband. Then, saying nothing, he handed the pillowcase to Elena, bent down, and kissed her on the forehead. It was then that she saw what she found hard to believe. There appeared to be a tear in her father's eye. However, the kiss was not held long enough for her to be certain, as he quickly turned and walked away.

"It is indeed our pleasure to have you with us, dear," Simone intoned, as she laid her hand gently on Elena's shoulder and moved her inside. "You may not think so now, but you'll soon be very glad you came."

Eleana looked around in awe. Based on what she was used to, she had just entered a palace.

*   *   *

Russell badly needed a shave, shower, and sleep. He opted, however, to go down to the beach first to see if any new eggs had been laid or hatchlings emerged. Throughout his walk along the sand, though, his thoughts kept careening from one female to the next. He was sad but thankful that he and Anne had one last opportunity to make a proper break and say goodbye. He was concerned about the degree of fear Elena had shown when the police burst into his cabin. Some shock was understandable, as was concern about her upcoming fate. But shock and concern weren't what he remembered seeing in Elena's eyes. It was terror pure and simple. And he wasn't sure why. There was also Inez. What had gotten into her? She must have mistaken his situation with Anne, but what set her off before that? He was determined to find out.

An hour later, Russell had completed the shave and shower but had blown off the idea of sleep. Instead, he went directly to Inez's flat. He could have called first, but he was afraid she might simply hang up on him. He hoped that if he showed up in person she'd be less likely to turn him away without at least some discussion. Now that he was actually knocking on her door, he was unsure if he'd made the right decision.

"Yes. Who is it?" Inez asked from inside.

Russell didn't answer. He just politely knocked again.

Ignorant as to who was there, she said, "If you're selling something, I don't want to buy. If you're panhandling, I don't have any money. If you have a package for me, or something like that, just leave it at the door."

Once again, Russell's only response was another knock.

"Oh, all right," Inez finally said and began opening the door. When she recognized who was there, she quickly tried to close it.

Russell got his foot between the door and the frame first, saying, "This is the uninjured one. Any chance of keeping it that way?"

"I can't believe you had the balls to come here," Inez snapped.

"Well, the fact that I'm here must mean my balls are still

intact—though I'm not sure about my other foot and my jaw—
and I really want to talk about what's bugging you."

"You're not going to stand there and tell me you have no
idea?"

"I have a very good idea, but I also have an idea that you've
misconstrued things."

"Oh, really."

"Yes. Really."

"So I've misconstrued things and the jailbird is going to set
me straight, huh?"

"You know about me being in jail?"

"Everybody knows about it. This is Retiro de Santos."

"I can explain that, too, but I'd rather do it inside."

Inez was momentarily silent. Russell took the opportunity
for one more appeal. "Just let me come inside to explain. If you
don't like the explanation, or you don't believe me, then you
don't even have to kick me out the door. You can just throw me
through the window."

Inez rather liked that particular scenario, so she opened the
door and let him in.

Russell decided to begin with what he knew. Inez had seen
Anne with him in the hotel. He told her who she was, went into
detail about their history, and let her know that he had no idea
she was coming to Retiro de Santos. Then he went on to say that
they had a long talk about their relationship and decided it was all
past and no future. He informed Inez that Anne left the next day.

"Did you sleep with her?" Inez asked.

"No," Russell said. "And yes."

In his effort to be completely honest, he told her that he and
Anne had indeed shared the hotel bed, but that they didn't share
each other. She said she believed him.

"Great," Russell said. "Now, let's get to what happened before you saw me with Anne. Why the hell did you punch me?"

Inez recounted going to his place and finding Elena in his bed. Was he going to deny that, she asked? No, he wasn't, he said. Then he went on to reiterate his relationship with Elena, her curiosity about the turtles, the fact that she was being made to work for Simone, and the concern he still had for her, especially the way she reacted when Delgado and his henchman broke in on them.

"Did you sleep with her?" Inez asked.

"No," Russell said. "Not really." Then he went on to explain how he used the cot on the nights Elena slept at his place.

The look in his eyes, the tone of his voice, his admission that even with the trouble he'd gotten into, he was still concerned about Elena—it all combined to make Inez believe him. She realized that she had overreacted, for which she apologized. He accepted her apology and offered his own for not trying to explain things sooner. But because he didn't bring it up, she didn't volunteer what she was thinking—that perhaps her conversation with Bennett led to Delgado learning of the girl's location. And because she didn't ask, he didn't tell her the real reason he stopped his pursuit of teaching, left Oklahoma, joined the WCO, and came to Retiro de Santos in the first place. Perhaps that conversation would come some other day. Perhaps. For now, that remained only between Russell and his unrelenting conscience.

Chapter 31

One day slid into the next quietly, as they had a tendency to do under the island's hot sun, cool nights, and occasional rain. When a week had passed without Elena dropping by his place, Russell's concern for her welfare grew. He didn't know where she lived, whether she was still at home, or had already been sent to Simone's. While he desperately wanted to know if she was okay, he was hesitant to take the initiative and find out. His continued concern for her could always be twisted by someone like Delgado, to make it appear his interest went far beyond friendship. And while his short incarceration and the resulting rumors and gossip had already gone a long way to making a lot of people believe the relationship between the local girl and the conservationist was more than platonic, he was in no hurry to dial up the heat on the hot mess his public profile had become. Yet still, he felt the need to do something.

*   *   *

Friday and Saturday nights were the busiest times at Simone's. More tourists joined the various shopkeepers, white-collar technicians, and blue-collar tradesmen who would sample the merchandise, make a selection, and eventually end their night feeling both satiated and sanguine. By and large, customers exhibited a spirit of frivolity, which Simone encouraged. Their behavior with the working girls—at least downstairs—was one of respect, which Simone's bulky overseer, Mateo, made sure of. All in all, the place felt a bit like a social club with the added benefit of carnal conviviality. There was no shortage of repeat business.

Elena had spent her time at the dwelling washing dishes, doing laundry, cleaning rooms, and getting to know everyone. The working girls adopted her right away. Many saw in her a younger sister, and each in her own way imparted knowledge about the care and feeding of customers hungry for more than hors d'oeuvres. Elena listened to their stories in silence, her trepidation obvious. So much so that more than one approached Simone suggesting that care be taken with the madam's choice of the young girl's first encounter. Simone was not dismissive of their entreaties, but neither was she immune to the realization that a premium could be placed on such a pristine prize.

*   *   *

Having secured the increased funding demanded by the consortium, Bennett was now in the process of letting contributors know that efforts were underway to lobby lawmakers regarding the disposition of the sanctuary beach. There had been no shortage of public information and private insinuation regarding the alleged scurrilous behavior of the World Conservation Organization employee and the rescued local girl. Therefore a combination of clandestine financial incentives and manufactured moral outrage were enabling more lawmakers to lend a sympathetic ear to lobbyists.

At the scenic overlook, two miles beyond the town square, Bennett stood smoking a cigarette. An old, but clean and shiny Lincoln pulled off the road and parked nearby. Mateo got out of the car and walked to where Bennett was admiring the view. The plantation owner offered the big man a cigarette. He accepted it and as he began to enjoy the tobacco while scanning the sea and the sky and the mountains, Bennett walked to the car and got in the backseat where Simone was waiting.

"Lovely day, isn't it Leland?"

"Indeed. I never tire of the view here. It always seems to comfort me in some way."

"Yes, we are truly blessed to live in such an idyllic environment."

"And speaking of blessings... I wanted to let you know that efforts are underway to pursue a favorable outcome for our collective investment."

"That's good to hear," Simone replied. "I take it young Russell's public embarrassment is lending a bit of tarnish to the reputation of the WCO."

"It's certainly heading in that direction. Thackery's death, and now the rumors about Russell... individuals are often seen as a reflection of the corporation they represent."

"Let's hope that's the case here. How are your other contributors feeling?"

"Well, as you might expect, Delgado is taking victory laps."

"Yes, he got his picture in the paper and everything. Looked rather pleased with himself."

"Simone, I want to caution you again about our dear Comandante. As I told you before, we need him involved for political reasons, but an asset can turn into a liability if one is not careful."

"That's a half-pregnant warning if I've ever heard one. Tell me straight out, Leland. What worries you about him?"

"This stays just between the two of us, right?"

"You know it does."

"Well, it's his temper. A temper he keeps under wraps most of the time. But perhaps not always."

"What do you mean?"

"When the change was taking place between Thackery and Russell, I needed to know how it might affect the consortium's pursuits. Was Thackery aware of what was going on? Had he passed his knowledge or perhaps his suspicions on to Russell? When I voiced my concerns to Delgado, he said he'd look into it."

Bennett paused to pull his pack of cigarettes from his coat pocket.

"No smoking in the car, Leland."

"Oh, of course," he answered, putting the pack back in his pocket. "Nasty habit anyway."

"You were talking about Delgado and the Australian."

"Yes. Well, according to Delgado, Thackery said he knew there were some efforts afoot to pressure government officials in regard to the beach. When pressed, Thackery said he hadn't mentioned anything about it to Russell because he didn't want the new man to worry about things he had no control over. He told the Comandante that he was going to discuss what he knew directly with the WCO hierarchy. Delgado suggested that he keep whatever he thought he knew to himself. Apparently, the Australian told him what he could do with his suggestion. One insult led to another and things got out of hand. Delgado told me he was only going to rough Thackery up a bit. To show him who was boss. He said they scuffled. Thackery slipped, fell down the hill, and accidentally hit his head. Personally, I have my doubts about the accidental part."

Bennett paused slightly before continuing. "In retrospect, Thackery's death is beneficial to our cause as it is one more thing our lobbyists can use to sully the reputation of the WCO."

"How so?"

"Everyone who knew him knew Thackery was a big drinker. It isn't difficult to paint a picture that the Australian was complicit in his own demise."

"So one WCO employee is seen as an alcoholic, and another as an abuser of young women."

"Can an organization that hires such people be trusted, or allowed to continue its oversight of such an important property?"

"Leland, I never realized just how devious you really are!"

"Well, just keep in mind how volatile Delgado can be. We don't want to do anything that might cause his impulsiveness to interfere with our plans."

Simone reached over and took Leland's hand in hers. "Thank you for sharing this with me. I've never cared for Delgado. My girls tell me he can be a pig. But you're right that we should have local law enforcement on our side. I'll heed your warning, Leland."

Chapter 32

Sunlight crept through the back window of the American's cabin, spilling its yellow glow across two bodies covered only by a thin sheet. Inez and Russell's relationship had returned to a semblance of what it was before her misconceptions and his run-ins with the law. The night before had been spent with him bemoaning the apparent public embarrassment he had become, along with his continued concern for Elena's well-being. Inez had argued that no one's opinion about him mattered, except his own, and that he needed to accept the fact that there was nothing he could do for the young girl since her age made her young enough to still be legally beholding to her father but not too young to be illegally employed by Simone. When their exchange crossed over into legal and illegal versus right and wrong, both knew it was time to finish the wine and the conversation. But after their post-discussion coupling, both lay on the bed in the darkness adrift in individual contemplation. Russell exploring what he should or shouldn't do. Inez pondering what she should or shouldn't say.

After waking, morning found them at the beach. Russell had asked if Inez wanted to join him on his inspection and she did.

When they reached the boulders that bordered the south end of the beach, Inez's eyes grew wide.

"Ah! My God. Look at that."

Russell joked. "Look at what?"

"That!"

"Oh, that. That's only Minerva. She's probably coming back from breakfast."

The giant leatherback was emerging from the surf and slowly making her way toward the huge rocks.

"She's spectacular," Inez gushed.

"Yes. She really is. Weighs in just under a ton. Likes it here. When she's not sea cruising, she likes to sidle up to those rocks over there. Sometimes you can't even tell one from the other."

"How old is she? Do you know?"

Russell replied. "You know it's not nice to ask a female her age. But she's forty-ish. Don't tell her I told you."

Holding out her hand, Inez asked, "I don't suppose I could…"

"I wouldn't advise it. Not sure how she might react. Some are not partial to strangers."

"What did you say her name was?"

"Minerva."

"Who came up with that?"

"Thackery. I asked him if that was the name of an old girlfriend… or maybe the one that got away."

"What did he say?"

"Said there were too many of the latter and not enough of the former. So according to him, he just looked her in the eye until a name came to him."

"And the name was Minerva?"

"That's what he said."

"Do you think she misses him? Thackery, I mean."

"I'd like to think so," Russell answered. "Out here, alone

with her once, I told her what happened to him."

Inez was touched by what he said, and the fact that he actually did it. "A loner who talks to turtles. You're a strange one, Stephen Russell. Strange in a good way." Then she took him by the arm and kissed him on the cheek.

"Hey, better watch that. She might get jealous."

"Don't worry, Minerva. I'm not trying to take him away from you. He's man enough for both of us."

The giant turtle gave no sign of agreeing or disagreeing, but simply continued her slow trek toward the rocks.

*   *   *

It is said that the best advertising is word of mouth. Certainly in a community the size of Retiro de Santos, that assertion is more truth than cliché. Anyway, Simone thought, to partake in something more publicly overt could easily be seen as crass or vulgar and would not substantially increase the number of attendees. Better, she thought, to simply let Mateo spread the word through his network of friends and compatriots. They in turn would divulge the information to their own acquaintances, and before long virtually every male on the island would know that a non-lethal virgin sacrifice was to be conducted at the big purple house this coming weekend.

An auction didn't feel quite right to Simone. She felt that was too exclusive for the proletariat and too improper for the bourgeoisie. The upper crust—what was left of it—wouldn't particularly care *how* the prize was won. If she was any judge, and she was, the swells would only be interested in the rareness of the event and their own odds of coming out on top. If that was the position they preferred.

She eventually decided to go with a lottery of sorts. A

raffle where one could purchase no more than three chances. However, one had to be on-site to purchase and present to win. Thereby ensuring a large crowd and even larger liquor sales. It would be quite a night to remember, thought the mistress of the house. Perhaps even unforgettable for the winner, and certainly for Elena.

*   *   *

As expected, word of the impending event spread surreptitiously but rapidly. Response and intention to attend varied. A curious parishioner asked Father Alonzo how he felt about such a sordid event.

"Though certainly, I've never been to Simone's, I considered showing up, if for no other reason than to support Elena. But they would not let me in. Simone would see my presence as detrimental to the atmosphere of frivolity she wants to create. She would have Mateo keep me at bay. All I can do is pray now and hear confessions later."

A business associate queried Bennett, who responded, "I'll be there. Not necessarily to participate, but to observe. There is less and less to do in Retiro de Santos that stimulates both the mind and the body. Perhaps the night will prove interesting."

Delgado's underling asked and was answered. "Of course, I will attend. Such an event needs oversight. It is my responsibility to make sure peace, as well as amusement, is maintained. And who knows, I might try my luck as well."

After reaching a decision in his own mind, Russell was ready to answer Inez.

"Are you going?"

"Yes. I realize no one made me her protector, I just don't want her to feel abandoned."

"But what can you possibly do about it?"

"Maybe I'll luck out and draw the winning chance. It could happen."

"And if so?"

"I know what you're thinking… and no, I'd never do that. I just want her to know there are still people who care about her. Do you believe me?"

"Strangely enough, I do."

"Good. Because it's too far to walk to Simone's from my place, so I was hoping I could borrow your scooter."

*   *   *

Simone made sure that Mateo doubled the amount of booze they normally stocked. The working girls spent additional time sprucing up their own rooms plus the common areas as well, realizing that most of those who played but lost would not want to leave without some sort of satisfaction. Elena did her best to maintain composure as she was schooled in makeup, demeanor, technique, and importantly, post-coital behavior. Advice from the pros was free-flowing. Just close your eyes and bear it one told her. Another said that it wouldn't take long, especially if the winner was older. A third suggested that if the man was handsome, she might even enjoy it. Stranger things had been known to happen.

Elena however, was no less averse to her predicament than she always had been, but she slowly came to rationalize that, for whatever reason, God had left her in this place with these people. Therefore her only choice was to accept it. She knew her innocence would soon be lost, but perhaps she'd be able to hang onto something she cared even more about—hope.

Chapter 33

The night began as most before it. When the sun went down, a light on the porch came on indicating that Simone was open for business. One by one the house began to fill with customers. Before the crowd became too large, each arrival was introduced to any of the girls he had not met previously. This included Elena, who was dressed differently from the other women in the house. They were all draped revealingly in dresses with high slits and low necklines. She was attired in what Simone thought of as Catholic school finery—a white blouse buttoned at the throat, black skirt ending just above the knees, and thigh-high socks running into patent leather shoes. The only things that seemed to be missing were the blazer and the schoolbooks, but even Simone felt that might be a tad too much. Just enough makeup had been applied to accent her full lips and dark eyebrows. Her hair fell to her shoulders along with her mood. When she was introduced to various men, she would force something resembling a smile before her head and eyes turned to the floor. Shy was the word Simone used to describe her in each greeting, along with a phrase she felt appropriate for the occasion.

"Good evening, Simone."

"Good evening, Leland. So nice to see you. I don't believe you've met the newest member of our happy family. Elena, say hello to Mr. Bennett."

A forced smile. The drop of her head as she recited stoically, "Good evening."

"Good evening to you, Elena. You look quite lovely this evening. Has Simone been treating you well?"

Her eyes remained on the floor as she nodded her head affirmatively.

"She's very shy," Simone explained unnecessarily, before moving on to the next guest.

After a few more introductions, Simone saw that the long, and often heavy-handed arm of the law had arrived. Mateo met him at the door and granted entry. Taking Elena by the hand, Simone was walking toward the policeman when the girl stopped in her tracks.

"What's the matter, love? It's only Comandante Delgado."

Elena didn't answer. But her feet stayed glued to the floor.

Delgado spotted the two and walked over. "Hello, Simone. Quite a gathering this evening. And hello again, Elena. You remember me. I brought you home to your father."

A head nod came in response. Simone could feel the girl trembling.

"Such a big night, Comandante. I'm afraid Elena is a bit overwhelmed."

"Understandable," the policeman began, "I am sure she will become accustomed to being the center of attention as time goes by."

"No doubt," Simone answered, and she would have said more, but just then Elena let go of her hand and raced across the room.

"Stephen, you came!" Elena said, reaching out and grasping both of Russell's hands.

"Yes. How are you? Are you okay?"

"Well…"

"Have they been treating you well?"

"They have all been very nice. But you know what they expect of me… tonight?"

Before he could answer, Simone, with Mateo behind her, joined them.

"Mr. Russell. Nice of you to come. I believe this is your first visit to our establishment."

"Yes. It is."

"Well, since you already know Elena, perhaps you'd like to meet some of our other girls."

"Not right now. I just want to have a word or two with Elena."

"I'm afraid that's not possible at the moment. She has to prepare. Please, have a drink. Everyone is having a good time. Enjoy yourself."

Russell was about to respond, but Mateo stepped between him and Simone as she took Elena by the hand and led her away. The American didn't argue. He hadn't come to start a row. He wasn't exactly sure why he had come. But if he couldn't help Elena, *what was the point*, he asked himself.

A table had been set up near the bar. It was manned by Carla, one of Simone's most loyal and profitable staff members. Atop the table was a sign reading:

WIN THE RIGHT
TO WELCOME
THE NEWEST MEMBER
OF OUR FAMILY.

Chances, in the form of tickets, each with its own individual number, cost one hundred dollars. No one was allowed to buy more than three. Customers had been purchasing them all evening. Bennett had chosen to abstain. Delgado bought one chance. Though he couldn't really afford it, Russell bought three. *At least*, he thought, *I will have done all that I can.*

Simone had taken Elena up to room seven. She tried as best she could, to put the frightened girl at ease.

"Just sit here and wait, dear. The drawing will be soon. A gentleman will come to your room. You will become a woman soon. It's not as difficult or terrible as you think. Tomorrow it will simply be a memory of yesterday. Mateo and I will be nearby should you need us. But I'm sure you will not. Try to relax, love. You are a beautiful girl. Many will gladly pay to be with you in the days ahead. You will make lots of money for you and your family. It all starts tonight."

Twenty minutes later, the patrons were advised that it was time for the drawing. The room quieted, as best a room full of libidinous drinkers is able. Simone stepped to the table and spoke to the crowd.

"I want to thank you all for participating. The girls and I welcome your enthusiasm and your compensation. Not necessarily in that order."

Laughter rippled through the gathering.

She continued. "All of the tickets are in this vase Carla is holding. I will draw one ticket and call out the number. The winner is free to let everyone know he is triumphant, or he may keep his victory to himself, and see me quietly to gain access to his prize. With no further ado…"

Simone kept her eyes on the crowd as she reached into the vase and pulled out one ticket.

"The winning number is 358694. Once again, that's 358694."

A high-pitched and excited voice came from the back of the room. "That's my number. I think that's my number!"

"Then, come, let me see it," Simone responded.

The group of men parted to make way for a slight fellow wearing a three-piece suit and wire-framed glasses. When he'd made his way through far more burly types to reach the front of the room and Simone, he said, "Here's my ticket. I think you called my number."

"Let me see," she said, taking it from him. "Your ticket is 3586..."

Her pause let the air out of the room, and the excitement out of the man.

"I'm sorry. Your ticket is 358654. Not 358694. I'm terribly sorry."

"*You're* sorry," the man said, followed quickly by the others' guffaws.

"Well then, no one wants to come forward now?" Simone asked. "All right, whoever has 358694, please see me later. And everyone else, well, feel free to enjoy yourselves upstairs or down... if you know what I mean... and I think you do."

Raucous laughter ensued. Ticket stubs were torn in half and thrown in the air. Conversation that had been muted rose in volume exponentially, and merriment once again prevailed. Simone continued to walk among the crowd playing her role as hostess. She was unaware that someone was following her, waiting for just the right moment. It came in a corner of the room, when she disengaged from one conversation and was beginning to walk to another. From behind, a hand reached out and tapped her on the shoulder. "I have the winning number," she heard a voice say. When she turned around, she saw a hand holding a ticket stub extended toward her. The hand belonged to Stephen Russell.

"358694," he said. "That's it, right?"

Simone took the stub and read the number. "Yes, that is it. Lucky you," she said, less than enthusiastically.

"So," Russell said, "what happens now?"

"Now, I give you the key to Room 7," she began, as she handed it to him. "Second floor. And please remember, she is a young girl, unaccustomed to the practice of pleasure." Then she paused slightly before adding, "Unless, of course, she acquired some skills from the time she spent with you."

Russell looked at her but said nothing. Then he turned and headed toward the stairwell.

Chapter 34

Elena heard the key going into the lock. She held her breath as she saw the doorknob turning. She didn't want to look, but she was afraid not to. Then the door opened and Russell stepped in.

"Stephen," she cried, rising from her chair and running to him. "I'm so happy it is you," she exclaimed, throwing her arms around him and hugging him tightly.

He responded by putting his hands on her shoulders and moving her back gently. When he did, he realized her eyes were filled with tears. "It's all right, Elena. Everything's going to be okay."

Choking back her sobs, she said, "I prayed, Stephen. I prayed it would be you. God must have answered my prayers."

"I don't know if it was God, or luck, or what, but I couldn't believe it myself when I realized I had the winning ticket."

Raising her hand and wiping a tear from her eye, she said, "So... does this mean that you and I—"

"No. It doesn't mean that."

"But if it has to be... I mean if it must... then I want the first time to be with someone kind and gentle. Like you, Stephen."

"You deserve someone kind, Elena. But it should be someone you really want to be with. Not someone that's being forced on you."

"But..."

"Just wait. I have a plan. I'm not sure it's a very good plan. But right now, it's the only one I've got. They'll probably leave us alone for a while. That might give us time."

"Time for what?"

Downstairs, the mood had begun to change from excitement to enticement. Simone's girls, highly skilled at the art of persuasion, were busily convincing those who didn't win the night's top prize to consider a pleasant alternative. The patrons were not hard to convince.

Though one or two had other things in mind.

"Simone," Bennett said, "did I see you talking to young Russell, earlier?"

"You did."

"Don't tell me—"

"He did. Can you believe the luck? I mean, I guess it doesn't matter in the grand scheme of things. I suppose he assumed that he missed his chance when he had her at his place. And this was an opportunity to make up for that."

"Odd. He never really struck me as the type," Leland said.

"The type for what?" The question came from Delgado, who had joined them in mid-conversation.

"The type to be so attracted to a very young woman," Leland began, "that he would continue to risk his, and his employer's reputations simply for sexual gratification."

"What? You mean that Russell had the winning ticket?"

"That's right, Comandante," Simone answered. "He's up there with her now."

"*Bastardo*," Delgado swore. "He is still facing a charge of obstructing justice and he comes here to be with her right under our noses. What *cajones* he has! I think it is time that I question him further. What room is he in, Simone?"

Bennett could tell the policeman had consumed a number of drinks. He didn't want things going too far. "I'm not sure that's a good idea."

"Why isn't it?" Delgado barked.

"Well, I'm sure Simone doesn't want it getting around that the police can just burst into her rooms while business is being conducted. That could put customers off."

Simone, recalling what Bennett had said to her about Delgado's temper, quickly added. "Leland has a point, Comandante."

"Still… I want to talk to him. Now. Hopefully, before he's finished. Perhaps it will ruin his evening. That would show him, would it not?"

"Why don't I check on them?" Simone volunteered. "It would not be out of the ordinary for me to find out if all is well. Then I can tell the young man that you want to speak with him when he comes down."

"Me? Wait for him?"

"I'm sure the fact that you want to talk with him will blunt his passion," Bennett injected. "It won't be long, and I will buy you a drink in the meantime."

"You will check on them now, Simone?"

"Yes, Comandante. Have a drink with Leland and I'll be right back."

Upstairs, Russell and Elena had begun to execute his last-minute plan. They had stripped the bed, tied the sheets together, affixed one end to the bedpost, and trailed the other out the window. Fortunately, the length was sufficient that only a small drop would be required to hit the ground. As the room was on the dark side of the house, chances were they wouldn't be seen.

"I'll go first," Russell said. "That way, if you should fall, I'll be able to catch you."

"But where will we go once we're out?" Elena asked.

"I have a destination in mind. But we must hurry. Come to the window and watch as I go down… so you'll know what to do."

She did as he said and saw him going out the window holding onto the sheet and letting his feet brace against the side of the house. Then he descended slowly, hand under hand, until he dropped the short distance to the ground.

"Come on," he said, looking up at her. "Just do as I did."

With her hands on the sheet, she was about to step out of the window when she heard a knock on the door and Simone's voice.

"Hello. Just checking to see if you need anything?"

Elena froze. She didn't know whether to keep going or stay. She didn't know whether to speak or remain silent. Simone spoke again.

"Hello. Is everything all right in there?"

Elena started to speak, then stopped herself. She wasn't sure what to say or do.

Again Simone spoke. "Elena? Mister Russell? Please answer. I need a response of some kind."

Elena made her decision. She swung one foot over the window sill.

Annoyed now that neither would answer, Simone took her universal pass key and opened the door. Shock hit her first. The bed was askew. Pillows and blankets strewn on the floor. No sheets on the bed. Momentarily confused, she looked over and saw Elena with one leg inside the room and the other out.

"What are you doing?" Simone shouted. "Get back in here!"

Rushing from the door to reach Elena, Simone's stiletto heel caught in a comforter on the floor, causing one shoe to be pulled off. Her momentum thrust her toward the window. Elena was too fearful to look back. She had gotten both legs outside and was starting down. Still stumbling forward and unable to stay upright, Simone fell and crashed headlong into the edge of the marble vanity top near the window. Blood immediately started to flow down the side of her face. Slumped on the floor against the vanity, she tried to reach up and touch her wound, but she didn't have the strength to raise her hand. Lights in the room appeared to go on and off as she slipped in and out of consciousness. Dizziness and nausea began to overwhelm her. She felt herself slowly drifting away, but somehow she managed to raise her eyes enough to see an immense, dark figure step into the doorway.

"Miss Simone!" Mateo shouted.

Chapter 35

Russell and Elena ran to the side of the house where several cars were parked. Beside an old Buick was the Moped he had borrowed from Inez. Straddling it, he said, "Hop on behind me and put your arms around my waist."

She did as he instructed. Then he kick-started it and they raced off into the night. Elena had never been on a scooter before. She was both frightened and exhilarated. Clinging to Russell, she hung on for dear life as he tilted the two-wheeler and leaned into each curve. Neither was aware of what had transpired with Simone, but both assumed that someone would soon be looking for them. Russell pressed the scooter for all the speed it could muster. He hoped it would be sufficient to keep him ahead of any pursuers long enough to reach his destination. And he hoped even more that *where* he was going was the right place to go.

After fifteen minutes of high-speed maneuvers over the twisting, turning road, they rounded a curve and Russell saw what he was looking for. Lights were on in both the church and the rectory. He drove the scooter to the unlit area between the two, then turned off the motor, took Elena by the hand, and hurried to the door. It was unlocked. They stepped inside the church and saw Father Alonso at the altar. As the two raced up the center aisle, the sounds of their scurrying steps caused the priest to turn.

"Elena. Señor Russell. What are you doing here?"

Still winded, Russell blurted. "Father, Elena seeks sanctuary."

"What do you mean?" The priest asked.

"Sanctuary, father. Sanctuary. This is a church, right? And churches provide sanctuary to people in need. Elena needs sanctuary."

Looking at the girl, Father Alonso asked, "Is this so, little one? Do you seek the sanctuary of the church?"

Elena looked quickly to Russell who nodded his head.

"Yes, Father," Elena said. "I seek sanctuary."

The priest intoned, "This is not something to be done lightly, child. There must be a good reason for you to lay yourself at the mercy of the church."

Elena looked at the priest. Then at Russell. She wasn't sure what to say. Russell jumped in. "She's just come from Simone's. She was being auctioned off like... like... livestock."

Elena quickly joined in. "Yes, Father. At Simone's. They were making me—"

"Enough, child," the priest interrupted. "If you truly want sanctuary, you must admit your sins the right way. Come, let us move to the confessional."

Father Alonso moved to take Elena's hand, asking Russell, "You will be here when we finish?"

"Yes. I'll wait and try to figure out what *I* should do next. But she'll be able to stay here, right?"

"If she truly is seeking sanctuary, I will do what I can to provide it."

"And you don't have to tell anyone that she's here? Correct?"

"I don't have to volunteer it," the priest said. "If I am asked, that may be another matter."

"Thank you, Father."

"Are you sure that you wouldn't like to confess as well?"

"Uh, no. No, I don't think so. I'll just wait here while the two of you... you know. I might pace for a bit. Sometimes I think better on my feet. Will it be long?"

"I think not," Father Alonso replied. Then turning to Elena, he said, "Come child."

Russell began to walk up and down the aisles as the two went into the confessional.

"Bless me, Father, for I have sinned. It has been three weeks since my last confession."

The priest knew Elena had been at Simone's since she was last in church. He made an assumption regarding what he was about to hear. His assumption was wrong.

"Father, I'm not sure what you want me to tell you. Since my last confession, I have not disobeyed my mother or father, and I have not fought with my brothers."

"Elena, you know what sin is. And you know where you have been. So you can tell me."

"But Father, I did not commit any sins there. I did what I was told and I did not fight or disobey anyone."

"But Elena, if they had you lie with men—"

"Oh, I did not do so, Father! I mean... I was going to, I guess, but Stephen... Mr. Russell... he got me out of there before I had to be with anyone."

"He did? Before you were with any man?"

"Yes. And then he brought me here... hoping the church would grant me sanctuary, so I wouldn't have to be with anyone or do anything."

"Well, if your conscience is clear, and you feel you have not sinned in any way…"

"May I ask a question, Father?"

"Of course, my child."

"Father, is it a sin *not* to do something? Something that you think you should?"

"That depends. If you know that by *not* doing something, it might cause harm… that might be sinful."

"Father, I saw a terrible thing."

"I can imagine. Terrible things go on at Simone's."

"No. It was not at Simone's. It was before I was taken there."

"Oh. Well, you should go ahead and unburden yourself. What was this terrible thing?"

Russell's pacing had already enabled him to make one loop around the inside of the church. As he was about to pass the confessional, he could hear their voices. He had not planned to eavesdrop, but Elena's next words transfixed him.

"I saw a man killed."

"What?" Father Alonso began. "You saw a man killed? Did you know this man?"

"It was the man called Thackery. The man who helped the turtles before Stephen."

"Oh, I see. You saw his accident. You saw him trip and fall? That must have been awful for you. But you have not committed a sin by not telling anyone."

"You do not understand, Father. He did not trip. It was not an accident. I saw a man hit him, and push him down the mountain."

"Elena… are you sure? Are you sure of what you saw?"

"I am very sure, Father. I have not been able to get it out of my head since that day."

"And… the man who hit and pushed him…do you know this man?"

"I did not know him when I saw him do it. But later, when he came to Stephen's cabin and found me there. I realized it was the same man."

"The same man?"

"Yes. It was the policeman. The one called Comandante Delgado."

"¡*Madre de Dios*!" Father Alonso said involuntarily. "How did you see this?"

"I was on the mountainside, watching the beach below as I had done many times before. I heard noises coming my way. Men talking. So I hid in the tall grass and bushes. They never saw me. But I saw them. And I saw what the man, Delgado, did."

"And you have told no one of this? Not your parents? Or… Señor Russell… or anyone?"

"No. I was afraid. Afraid to tell. But then I became fearful that I was doing wrong. What if he hurts someone else, I thought. Would I be responsible? For not telling what I know. Was my silence a sin, Father?"

There was a long pause before the priest answered. Outside the confessional, Russell was initially stunned but not entirely surprised. He had always thought Thackery had too much mountain goat in him to simply lose his balance and fall. Now he knew the truth. But what was he to do about it? It was too much to process quickly, so he moved past the confessional, not wanting them to know that he had been listening.

Father Alonso finally said, "Elena, I must give this some thought. You have not sinned, but we need to think wisely about what to do next. I will try to make it possible for you to stay in the church and the rectory until we work this out."

"Thank you, Father."

"But… just to be on the safe side, go ahead and say ten Our Fathers and ten Hail Marys."

Chapter 36

Delgado let Bennett buy him not one drink but two. Then he tired of waiting. The liquor had not mollified his anger as Bennett hoped it would. If anything, it only served to increase his resentment toward Russell, this gringo who thought he could do what he pleased while flaunting authority. Without a word to his tablemate, he stood abruptly, crossed to the stairs, and headed up to find the American. Reaching the second floor it occurred to him that he had no idea which room Russell and the girl might be in. But looking around, he saw that one of the doors was open. He hurried to it. Stepping inside he saw the bed that was stripped, the sheet that was hanging out the window, and he saw Mateo on the floor holding the fallen Simone in his lap. When the big man looked up and saw the policeman, he said, "She's gone."

"Gone?" Delgado asked.

"She's dead," Mateo answered.

Enraged, the still-drunk Delgado didn't wait to hear any more. He bolted back into the hall, then raced down the stairs and out the front door. His VW Iltis had been parked so no other vehicle could block his exit. He immediately slid in the driver's seat, cranked the engine, and with tires spinning and gravel flying, peeled into the night.

*   *   *

Russell didn't tell Father Alonso or Elena that he had overheard what she said about Comandante Delgado. He simply said that he had to go and that he would check with them the following day... maybe... if he wasn't jailed for kidnapping again... or perhaps theft since Elena was probably looked upon somehow as Simone's property in the topsy-turvy legal world of Retiro de Santos.

As he walked back outside to the parked scooter, Russell knew the authorities would be looking for him, but he told himself he could probably stay unseen at Inez's place for a day or two until he figured out exactly what to do. Since he had come up with no other alternative, it seemed a reasonable idea. He hoped he wouldn't be putting her at risk for harboring a fugitive, but he could always say she had no knowledge of where he'd been or what he'd done. There was no way anyone could prove otherwise if they both stuck to the same story. Then he began to wrestle with whether or not he should tell Inez about Delgado. Would knowing put her in danger? Would not knowing be safer? At this point, he wasn't sure. The only thing he was sure about was that he needed some time to think things through. Hopefully, he could get that time at Inez's. So he straddled the scooter again, revved it up, and took off for her place, having no idea what had happened to Simone and that potential charges against him might also include murder.

*   *   *

Delgado headed directly to Russell's cabin. Clearly, it would have been foolish for the American to go home after running off with the girl. But clarity wasn't part of Delgado's thought processes at that moment. He was thinking with a mind full of liquor and a heart full of hate. *Damn Americans*, he reflected as he drove. *They all think they're better than us. One will soon learn that is not the case.*

He pushed his makeshift jeep for all it had. Soon he was screeching to a halt on the side of the road beneath Russell's cabin. The policeman gave no thought to stealth or safety. He jumped out of his car, bounded up the stone path leading to the porch, raced up the stairs, and in one violent move, kicked in the door that had recently been repaired after having been rent asunder from the previous police visit.

Delgado stood in the doorway looking around. He saw no one. But he heard some sort of sound coming from the closet. Removing his revolver from its holster, he walked across the living area with gun in hand. Pausing momentarily in front of the closet door, he once again heard sounds. They sounded as if someone was scratching—scratching at the door trying to get out. Bracing his feet, the policeman prepared himself. Then he reached out, put his hand on the knob, and quickly yanked the door toward him. But just as quickly as the door flew back, a brown ball of fur with pointed nose and ringed tail leapt directly on Delgado's chest. Staggering backward and trying to knock the coatimundi off with his free hand, the perplexed policeman almost fell but managed to keep his balance. Just then the coati jumped off his chest, onto the floor, and headed directly for the kitchen. Delgado didn't think twice, or even once about what he was doing, he immediately raised his gun and fired two shots in quick succession at the offending animal. The first was low and put a hole in the stove. The second was high and shattered the window above the sink. Bolivar took advantage of the opening, sprung through what was left of shattered glass, and vanished into the darkness.

*   *   *

Russell was halfway to Inez's flat when another thought crossed his fevered brain. How long would he have to hide there? Maybe longer than he realized. Perhaps he should rush back to his place to gather a change of clothes and anything else he might need for an extended stay. He slowed the scooter to almost a stop, made a U-turn in the middle of the deserted road, then roared off toward his cabin. He'd be careful, he told himself, and make sure no one was there before he went in. He'd be quick, he determined, and grab only the essentials that were needed. He'd be in and out and then at Inez's before anyone could figure out where he might be. At least that's what he thought at that moment. His mind continued mulling alternatives as he roared down the deserted road.

Delgado had gone back to his vehicle and driven away from Russell's place as swiftly as he had driven to it. He decided to go to town to pick up more firepower, and maybe even Garza, if the fat *cerdo* hadn't abandoned his post and gone home by now. With his own addled brain trying to shake the alcoholic cobwebs away, he saw a single light coming toward him on the road. Assuming it was just another car with one headlight out, he swung halfway out of his lane and onto the shoulder to let it pass. In doing so, he had to keep his focus on navigating his own off-road maneuver, and didn't recognize the individual on the scooter that sped past him.

Until then, Russell had the two-lane blacktop to himself. Traffic in and out of Retiro de Santos never being heavy, at this time of night, it was practically a ghost road. But there was no imagining the one-of-a-kind vehicle veering to the side of the road to give him room he obviously didn't need. *"My God. Delgado!"* Russell said to himself. He turned his head just enough so he could make out whether the policeman had recognized him and was turning his car around to give chase. He wasn't. Once again, mental gymnastics kicked in. He had no idea if the thought that popped into his head was good or bad, but he slowed the scooter anyway, U-turned again, and headed after Delgado. *If I can find out what he's about to do, without him seeing me, I'll have a better idea of how to avoid him longer.* That was the extent of Russell's tortured planning as he turned off the scooter's headlamp and let moonlight guide his rush toward the fading taillights of Delgado's vehicle.

Chapter 37

The church was between Russell's cabin and the police station in the center of Retiro de Santos. As Delgado was about to pass the house of worship on his way to retrieve his deputy, he noticed that the lights were still on. Slamming on the breaks, he made a quick decision to let the priest know what had happened and to be on the lookout for Russell and the girl. He reasoned that the more people who knew what transpired at Simone's, the better chance he'd have of catching the duo. Once his vehicle had slowed enough, he pulled off the road and parked near the front of the church. Exiting his car, he walked quickly to the door of the church and entered.

Russell had made up enough ground that he saw Delgado entering the church. When the policeman closed the door behind him, the American piloted the scooter to the back side of the church, between it and the rectory. He then dismounted, went up the steps, and slipped in the back door. He found himself in an anteroom behind the proscenium. Crossing to the front of that enclosure, he found the entrance to the main part of the church. By positioning himself there, he was out of sight but within hearing distance of the conversation that had already begun.

"Why are you stopping here so late, Comandante?"

"Father, I need to inform you of recent events and ask that you watch for two fugitives."

Delgado's statement let Russell know that Elena wasn't out there. Or at least any place the policeman could see her.

"Fugitives?" Father Alonso asked. "Has someone done something wrong?"

"Indeed, Father. The worst thing imaginable. A murder has been committed."

Murder? What the hell is he talking about, Russell said to himself.

"Murder? How terrible. Who was the poor victim?"

"I regret to inform you, Father, it was Simone."

What, Russell silently gasped. *What's going on?*

"Simone. But how and where?"

"She was struck on the head, Father. At her place of business."

"How awful. And who are these fugitives? The ones you think did this?"

"I do not think, Father, I know. It was the American, Russell. And Elena Esperaza."

Russell was dumbfounded. He couldn't imagine what he was hearing. Something was incredibly wrong.

"Comandante, I can't believe Elena could have anything to do with this."

"She may not have... but she vanished from Simone's with Russell... who I am sure is responsible."

While incredulity was buffeting Russell's mind, Father Alonso's was working overtime. Could this be true? Why hadn't Elena or Russell said anything about it? And what about Elena's confession regarding Delgado? Was that true? Or were the girl and the American trying to deflect responsibility from themselves by making up a story about the policeman?

"But how do you know this about Russell? Did you see him do this thing?"

"I didn't have to see it. Russell and the girl were the only ones in the room," Delgado said. "Simone went up to check on them. When I went to look in on her, she was dead. There can be no other explanation."

Elena, who had been hiding behind the lectern, couldn't take it any longer. She broke past her fear with a burning need to defend Russell and make Father Alonso believe her. Bolting upright, she came around the lectern and said, "You lie! Stephen had nothing to do with anything like that."

Delgado was shocked. Why was the girl here? And was she alone?

"What is she doing here, Father? Is Russell here as well?"

"So many things happening," Father Alonso began. "So much being said. It is hard to know what… or who to believe."

For the moment, Russell stayed quiet. But there was no silencing Elena.

"Father, you must believe me. You must!"

"One would expect the young girl to lie about Russell. She is obviously enamored with him," Delgado offered.

"No, Father, I am not lying. Not about Stephen. And not about him. He… he is the killer I told you about in confession. I would not lie in confession."

"What are you talking about?" Delgado asked, addressing Elena.

"I told him about you. I saw you. I saw you hit and push Señor Thackery. And I told Father Alonso what I saw."

Delgado was taken aback. But his surprise quickly turned to subterfuge, and he responded, "Father, she is obviously making up a story. A story to gain your sympathy. It is her way to avoid responsibility for what happened to Simone."

"Father, believe me. We did not know anything about Miss Simone. We were escaping when she came into the room. There was no way we could have hurt her."

The priest looked from Elena to Delgado and back again. His brain was considering one thing, but his heart another. He went with his heart.

"I believe her, Comandante. I believe Elena."

Delgado's inebriation was wearing off. His demeanor became more threatening.

"I do not care what you believe. *You* cannot repeat what she said. It was told to you in confession. The girl said so. And no one will believe *her* anyway. She has run away twice to be with the American. And now she is facing a charge of accomplice to murder. She has every reason to lie. I will take her with me. She will help me find Russell or she will be put in a cell."

"You cannot take her," Father Alonso said. "Elena has sought sanctuary in the church. And as you know, sanctuary is inviolate."

"I know no such thing, Father. Sanctuary may have been acceptable in the past. Today it is as outmoded as much of the other drivel the church expounds." Then he turned to Elena. "Now girl, you must come with me."

"No, Father!" Elena exclaimed. "I don't want to go with him. I am afraid."

The priest stepped in front of Delgado. "You must not do this. I will talk to her about surrendering via her own free will. To let higher authorities determine who is telling the truth."

"You know as well as I do, Father, that in Retiro de Santos, I am the authority. Now get out of the way."

Russell, hearing it all, was torn. Should he turn himself in to Delgado? The man was surely dangerous. He couldn't let

Elena be taken alone. Then an idea leapt into his brain. It was probably crazy, but there was no time for self-debate. As the priest, the policeman, and Elena continued to argue, Russell ran through the back door from which he had entered. He grabbed the scooter and with two hands quickly walked it up the steps and into the area where he had been hiding. Again he heard Delgado's loud voice.

"Enough of this, priest. Step aside now. And don't run from me, girl."

Russell kick-started the Moped. The sound it made could easily be heard where the three were arguing, but it was incongruous, a strange noise that didn't belong in a house of worship. Russell, giving them no time to figure it out, gunned the engine and drove the scooter as fast as he could through the opening and onto the proscenium.

None of the three could believe their eyes, and Russell wasn't going to give them time to process what they were seeing. He sped past the lectern, over to and around the far side of the altar, and barreled down the center aisle of the church toward the front door.

"Stop!" Delgado shouted. "Stop now!"

Russell had no intention of stopping. He assumed that at least for the moment, the policeman wanted him more than he wanted Elena. He assumed correctly. Delgado began racing down the aisle to catch him, but the American only increased the speed of the scooter as it approached the two front doors. Both of which were closed. Surely they opened outward, he hoped, just before he banged into the one on the right. The force of the scooter knocked it open and he managed to stay atop the two-wheeler as it careened out the door, down the steps, and past the policeman's vehicle. *My God*, thought Russell, *it worked*. Delgado, with all the speed he could muster, abandoned the church, Father Alonso, and Elena, to chase the fleeing American.

Chapter 38

While there was no way the scooter could outrun Delgado's vehicle, it did have a distinct advantage. Russell could easily swing off the main road, hide behind a building or dense vegetation, and wait for the policeman to pass. Then if he wanted, he could scurry back on the blacktop and head in the opposite direction. The problem, however, was that Russell wasn't at all sure of what he wanted. His thinking thus far had only enabled him to get Delgado away from Elena. He was torn as to what his next move should be. He could go directly to Inez's flat to hide out, but having seen the scooter, the policeman might have recognized it as hers and could already be on his way to her place. He could go to someone else he knew. Perhaps someone like Bennett. He could explain what had happened and ask if he could hide there until more was known about Simone's death. Of course, that would put whoever helped him at risk of being charged with aiding and abetting someone in flight from the law. Certainly, he could not return to his cabin. That would be the first place authorities would look for him. But was that particular idea as insane as it sounded? What if it made sense to more or less hide in plain sight, stealing in and out of his cabin when he knew it was empty, and using the surrounding mountainside as camouflage to stay under cover when he knew searchers were nearby? A drowning man will clutch at whatever lifeline is thrown to him, and Russell was getting wetter by the minute. So he made the decision to swing back to his place, believing enough time had passed for Delgado to have searched there already.

When Russell was within a hundred yards of his cabin, he stopped the Moped and tried to see as best he could. Low-hanging clouds kept the moonlight and visual surveillance at a minimum. He could tell that no lights were on, but he couldn't remember if he was the one who turned them off before he left. He waited, just off the road and out of sight, for nearly half an hour. Long enough for him to convince himself that Delgado had come and gone. Which was half right.

With the scooter hidden behind overgrown grass and weeds near the side of the road, Russell dipped in and out of the shadows as he cautiously made his way to the cabin. When he reached the porch, he noticed that the door had been knocked in again, which gave support to his theory that police had come in hopes of catching him and had then been on their way. Trying to be sure, he peered in one widow and could see nothing in the dark. He then went ahead and stepped in through the open doorway.

Navigating the blackness on his way to the kitchen, he managed to arrive without tripping over anything or banging his shins. When he turned on the small light atop the stove, he noted the shattered window. Then he jumped and twitched simultaneously when he heard the voice behind him.

"Good evening, Señor Russell."

With his heart still pounding in his chest, Russell turned around and saw Delgado holding a gun.

"Jesus Christ! You scared the hell out of me."

"My apologies. I am sure your nerves are on edge after such a long and eventful night."

"You were here earlier, right? Then you came back."

"Yes," Delgado explained. "It was the first place I looked. Then after you managed to escape from the church, I knew it would be difficult to find you. So I decided to simply let you find me?"

"But why did you think I would come back here?"

"It seemed the worst possible thing for you to do. So I thought you might try it. One can always count on Americans to follow one mistake with another."

Russell let the insult slide, not only because the policeman was holding a gun, but also because there was a good deal of truth to what he said.

"I don't suppose it would do any good to tell you that neither Elena nor I know anything about what happened to Simone."

"You are correct. It would do no good whatsoever. It is what I would expect you to say."

"Well, maybe others will be more willing to listen to the truth."

"And what others would that be?"

"Whoever's going to hear my case. A judge? A jury?"

"One cannot believe what one does not hear," Delgado began. "I believe you Americans have a saying about that."

"Which would be?"

"Dead men tell no tales."

Russell didn't have to ask if the comandante was serious. But he felt his only chance was to keep Delgado talking.

"You'll have some sort of excuse for my death, I suppose."

"A simple shot-while-trying-to-escape will be more than sufficient."

"So… you'll have murdered me and Thackery, too. But why? What did either of us ever do to you?"

"You killed Simone, which is of course reprehensible, but actually, that should benefit us. Thackery was threatening to divulge our plans to his superiors. We couldn't have that."

"Wait," Russell implored, "Who is 'we'? What plans are you talking about?"

Delgado was about to tell Russell he'd have to die wondering when Bolivar made an unannounced return by leaping through the broken window. The moment startled both men but it also enraged one.

"Fucking coati!" Delgado yelled as he turned away from Russell and pointed his weapon at the scampering animal. The turn was Russell's chance. He shoved Delgado in the back as hard as he could and sent the policeman sprawling across the kitchen table. Then he dashed to the back door, flung it open, and hit the ground outside in full stride. Cursing the coatimundi and Russell and himself for being distracted, Delgado scrambled to his feet and took off after his fugitive.

Having lived there for weeks, Russell knew the trail's twists and turns well. He was able to negotiate the downhill path while moving at top speed. Delgado tried to hurry, but he knew if he went too fast he'd end up rolling rather than running down the hill. The space between them lengthened, but not enough to quiet the sound that Russell made rushing over stones, past ferns, and through tree limbs. At one point the American stopped and the sound of his descent came to a halt. When Delgado noticed there was now silence below him, he stopped also. But Russell had only been trying to gauge the length of his lead. When he stopped hearing the policeman's descent, he took off again. Delgado would have taken a breather, but when he heard Russell's dash renew, he quickly followed suit.

The events of that night had consumed both men so totally that neither noticed the first blush of pink sky preceding the dawn. Russell was running without any particular destination in mind. He was simply trying to get away from a man who wanted to kill him. Delgado was chasing with only one thought in mind, eliminate the man. But by the time he reached the bottom of the hill and the edge of the beach, the policeman was so winded he had to sit for a moment or lose his ability to breathe at all. As he sat taking in huge gulps of air, his chest moving in and out like a bellows, he scanned the beach in front of him. Somehow one breath became a chuckle. It was followed by another. The chuckle turned to a giggle which was quickly followed by full-throated laughter. Delgado sat and cackled as he stared out at what was in front of him. There, on the beach, were Russell's footprints. "*Estúpido, gringo,*" Delgado said to himself, realizing that if the American had run into the water to make flight, he'd have left no trail, making it impossible for his pursuer to know for certain whether to go right or left. But Russell had simply run down the beach leaving a primrose path to the rocks, where the tracks ended and he was surely hiding.

As he walked leisurely now, following the footprints in the sand, Delgado was thinking to himself that he'd need to finish Russell with one shot if it was truly to appear that the American had been killed while trying to escape. More than one wound might damage the credibility of that explanation. But he was not overly concerned. He had confidence in his marksmanship. Particularly at close range. Delgado's stroll to the boulders had also given him time to recalibrate how to achieve his desired end—a static target would be much easier to hit than one in motion—so he decided to lie.

"Señor Russell. Come out from these rocks. There is no need to hide. I have decided to take you in. It makes no sense to kill you. Capturing you and putting you on trial will help our cause even more. No one will believe you, and your organization will look even worse than it looks now."

Russell was still unclear as to what Delgado was talking about. What was *our cause*? Was the organization the WCO? Why did he want it to look bad? He didn't have answers to those questions, but he had to face the fact that he had run himself into a corner, and he certainly preferred the idea of not being killed. So he slowly rose and stepped to the side of the rock he had been hiding behind.

"Comandante, I think what you're saying is best for both of us." Then Russell lied too when he continued, "Anyway, Elena was probably mistaken. I'm sure she got overly excited and simply misconstrued what happened with Thackery."

The two were only a few feet apart now, and Delgado believed at this short distance his shot would be true. He broadened his stance slightly, brought his left hand up to brace his right, then sighted down the barrel.

"What are you doing?" Russell implored.

"Ending it," Delgado answered.

The policeman had been trained not to pull, but to slowly squeeze the trigger. Just as he was about to, the boulder he had been standing by moved, and the bones in his ankle cracked like nuts being shelled. The pain was so intense he cried out, fell, and fired a round that zipped past Russell, missing him by inches. Delgado continued to writhe and scream and fire his weapon as Minerva's jaws tightened even more around his shattered appendage. As the massive turtle sunk her spiky papillae in even deeper, the policeman stopped trying to hit Russell. Through incredible pain, he attempted to twist around so he could shoot the beast that had him in her vice-like grip. When the American saw what he was trying to do, he raced over and grabbed Delgado's gun hand, attempting to wrench the weapon away. Russell was struggling to dislodge the gun and pull the policeman free at the same time, but he wasn't accomplishing either. The harder Russell tried to pry the revolver from Delgado's hand, the tighter the man clung to it. The more Russell attempted to pull the policeman from Minerva's jaws, the tighter her grip became. Finally, the pain became so intense that Delgado screamed and passed out. Russell was pulling on the comandante's gun hand so hard that when consciousness left the policeman and his fingers went limp, the American's momentum caused him to tumble backward. Now, as he sat in the sand, he had the gun, but Minerva still had Delgado, and she was moving inexorably toward the outgoing tide.

Russell scrambled to his feet, put the gun in his waistband, and ran toward the macabre scene that was unfolding. The American had a decided advantage in speed. He reached them quickly, took hold of Delgado's arm, and tried to keep them from the water's edge. But the strength of the 170-pound American was no match for the strength of the almost-one-ton leatherback. With Minerva pulling one way and Russell the other, this was a tug of war he could not win. Her momentum began to tow Russell with them. Soon they would be in the surf. Russell knew the Comandante was unconscious but not dead. Yes, he was a son-of-a-bitch, the American realized, but he was also a human being. A human he now hated more than ever, because there was only one thing that Russell could do to save him. He gave one last tug with all the strength he could muster but it made no difference. All three were still heading toward the sea. Russell let go. He stood up and took the revolver from his waistband. Could he do it, he asked himself? Could he kill the very thing he had come here to help? All to save the life of a man who had planned to take his. But if he didn't, he pondered, would he be no better than the bastard that was being dragged away?

Russell looked at Minerva. The progeny of a species old as time. A creature who operates only on instinct, with no internal questions about good, bad, right, or wrong. Who was he, Russell questioned, to kill such a product of nature... perhaps such a product of God. But then, who was he if he didn't?

His eyes now wet with tears, feeling he simply had no other choice, Russell raised the revolver, pointed it at the head of the giant turtle, and pulled the trigger. Not once, but twice. Even a third time. And each time, there was a metallic click rather than a deafening crack. The gun was empty. Delgado had fired all six rounds. The American couldn't keep from asking himself, had Minerva been saved, or had he?

Russell stood at the water's edge and watched as the Leatherneck and the policeman slowly disappeared beneath the waves. How far would she take him? He realized it was impossible to know. Just as it was impossible to know why this night ended as it did. But the end had come, as it does to all nights. The American looked down at his hand still holding the gun. Then with all his might, he flung it as far as he could into the billowing surf.

Chapter 39

A week passed. Its first days found Delgado's deputy, the corpulent Officer Garza, mostly at wit's end. Where was his boss? No one seemed to know. What should he do? Initiative wasn't his strong suit. An anonymous phone call informed him that Delgado's vehicle was seen near Russell's cabin. He waited a day before having it towed to the station. When he learned there was to be a funeral in the middle of the week, he decided to attend, hoping perhaps someone might advise him on what to do next.

The ceremony for Simone was held at the church. It attracted a much smaller gathering than past weekends at her place of business. Staff was there, but very few customers. Father Alonso conducted a graveside ritual, though not a full mass. Elena, still under the mantle of sanctuary, was there. Leland Bennett attended and took it upon himself to suggest to Officer Garza that surely an inquest was needed to look into Simone's death, as well as the odd disappearance of Comandante Delgado. The deputy, relieved to get any directions for next steps, readily agreed and said he'd contact a Magistrate.

Inez was also at the remembrance. She had convinced Russell

not to come and to continue, at least for the time being, to stay holed up at her place where he had been for the last few days. Once the ceremony concluded and mourners were leaving, Bennett pulled Inez aside to speak to her.

"Inez," he began, "there's going to be a formal inquest into Simone's death and Delgado's disappearance. If you have any say in the matter—which I assume you do—you should do your best to have Russell... and probably the young woman also... voluntarily turn themselves in to the police before the proceeding. It will certainly make it look as if they're trying to be cooperative. And in the interim, I'm sure Officer Garza can be convinced to release them on their own recognizance. He seems an accommodating fellow."

"What makes you think I know where Stephen is?"

"My assumption is based on your overall demeanor. It's decidedly more content than it was in our last conversation. The one where you said you were going to listen to what Russell had to say about the women you found him with. I can only conclude you've reconciled."

"Well, perhaps we have... and perhaps I'll speak to him... if I see him, of course. But, if you have a moment, I'd like to talk to you about that matter we discussed *after* I whined about my love life."

"Certainly we can discuss it, love. But you should know, financially, that ship has sailed."

"I'm not trying to get my investment back, Leland. I'm just concerned about how it's being used."

"It's being used well, my dear. The game's definitely afoot."

"That's what I'm concerned about."

*   *   *

Russell was in the middle of his third cup of coffee when Inez returned from the funeral.

"So, how was it?"

"Low key. Not many people there. Simone's crew. A few others."

"Any more talk about… you know."

"Not overtly. Leland was there. He told me there's going to be an inquest."

"Formal?"

"Well, as formal as it gets here. You know the legal system isn't like it is in the states."

"How is it?"

"It's sort of a combination of tradition, customs, and civil law. This will probably be handled by what's called the Local Administrative Court of the First Instance."

"Wow. Long name. What's that *First Instance* mean?"

"It means, depending on how it goes, this could only be the first step before it gets bumped up to a higher court. Or not. It doesn't always happen that way."

"Did Bennett say when it was going to be?"

"He wasn't specific. But he did say he thought you and Elena should voluntarily turn yourselves in. To reinforce the fact you had nothing to do with Simone's death. He said Garza would probably release you until the inquest."

"He's probably right," Russell said. "Anyway, I don't like the idea of hiding and being on the run for something I didn't do. I'll talk to Elena. I'm sure she's frightened and wondering what to do next. What about you? What do you think?"

"I think the sooner it all gets cleared up, the better. I hate that you're having to go through this just because you were trying to help someone."

"Well, as they say, no good deed goes unpunished, right?"

"Since I haven't performed any good deeds lately, I really wouldn't know. And speaking of things we don't know, where do you think Delgado has gotten off to? This is the kind of thing he'd normally be right in the middle of."

Russell didn't answer. He had decided not to tell her of Delgado's fate because if things went bad for him, he didn't want Inez to have to admit she knew about Russell's role in the policeman's death, which might make her appear even more guilty of harboring a known criminal. And he didn't want to tell anyone about Delgado's role in Thackery's death without talking to Elena first. Was keeping knowledge from someone the same as lying about it? He hoped not, because that was what he was doing. He was unaware, however, that Inez was doing the same thing.

Chapter 40

The inquest took place in the hotel's euphemistically-named Great Room. While it was far from great, it was virtually the only place in the village large enough to hold the expected crowd. Attending the funeral of a known Madam may have proved too unsuitable for many of Simone's previous customers, but attendance at the investigation into her death was seen as much more civic-minded. Some even brought their wives.

Russell had taken the advice he'd been given and after talking with Elena, turned himself in to Deputy Garza. As expected, the conflict-averse policeman showed leniency and released the American on his own recognizance. Since Elena was staying at the church under the imprimatur of sanctuary it was deemed appropriate that she remain there until the inquest.

Magistrate Rudolfo Ortiz arrived to oversee the proceedings with not one, but two uniformed members of the Capital Policía. The Magistrate didn't anticipate disorder or unrest but his experience had shown that sometimes the unexpected happens, and he preferred to be safe rather than sorry. Ortiz himself was a slight fellow, bound tightly in a three-piece suit that anyone else would have found far too hot for the day. Thick spectacles sat atop the bridge of his thin nose and enabled his darting eyes to function almost normally. While he had coal black hair neatly trimmed on the sides and back of his head, one could run one's outstretched hand from his forehead to the top of his skull and never encounter a follicle. Magistrate Ortiz was one of those individuals whose appearance foretold his behavior. Both his look and his personality were punctilious.

Having called the meeting to order, the Magistrate began by having the village's lone doctor, who also served as coroner sans title, deliver an opinion on the cause of Simone's death. Blunt force trauma to the head was proffered by the medico and readily accepted by Ortiz who had a high regard for the medical profession and a low tolerance level for equivocation. The Magistrate elected not to probe further regarding the angle of assault or any other potentially complicating issues that might retard the pace of testimony. For Ortiz, a good inquest was a speedy inquest and he saw no reason to deviate from his modus operandi.

He next called for declarations from any who were in attendance at the fateful event that particular night. There was a decided lack of response, owing, no doubt, to the particular nature of the deceased's business. Once that request met with a deafening silence, the Magistrate moved on to the witness list Deputy Garza had provided. There were only three names on it, Elena Esperaza, Father Alonso, and Stephen Russell. Elena was called first and questioned directly by Ortiz.

"Were you an employee of Simone Tejeda?"

"Yes."

"Are you a prostitute?"

"No."

"Have you ever been a prostitute?"

"No."

"Were you in training to be a prostitute?"

"Well, yes."

"When were you to begin accepting clients?"

"That evening."

"And did you?"

"Yes… and no."

"Was it yes, or was it no?"

"Yes, one… client, as you say… came to see me. But we didn't do anything."

"Anything of a sexual nature?"

"That's right. Nothing of a sexual nature."

"Then what did you do?"

"We took the sheets off the bed, tied them together, and escaped through the window."

"Why did you do this?"

"Because I didn't want to be a prostitute."

"Did you hit this Simone in the head?"

"No. I did not."

"Did you attempt to kill this Simone?"

"No. I escaped through the window. I did not touch her."

"Are you lying?"

"No, I am not lying."

"I will be the judge of that."

"Please, ask Father Alonso. He will tell you I am not lying."

"I will call the Priest."

"Ask Señor Russell. He will tell you what he heard me say."

"I will call Señor Russell."

"One more question. And remember, when you testify in my proceeding, you are under an oath from God. Are you in love with this Russell?"

Elena didn't respond immediately. She paused, looked down at her lap, and said, "Sí. A little."

"You are excused," Ortiz barked. "Return to your seat. I now call Father Alonso."

The priest walked up and took the witness chair.

"You are Father Alonso?"

"I am."

"You are the priest for the village of Retiro de Santos?"

"I am."

"You know Elena Esperaza?"

"I do."

"You heard her say that you can confirm she is telling the truth."

"I believe she is telling the truth."

"In the church, what you believe is important. In this proceeding, what I believe is important. Can you confirm that she is telling the truth?"

"Unfortunately, no."

"Why not?"

"The Catholic Church does not allow it?"

"Does not allow what?"

"Does not allow me to discuss what I have discussed with Elena."

"And why is that?"

"Because of how… and where we discussed it."

"Are you implying she told you this in confession?"

"I cannot talk about anything relating to Elena and confession."

"Then you are of no help. To her, or to me. You may retake your seat."

As Father Alonso rose and headed back to his chair, his heart was heavy. He had done what was expected of him by his church, but what he hadn't done for Elena and Russell weighed on him. A murmur could be heard in the audience. Muffled questions were asked of one another. Why wouldn't the priest support her? Where was this leading? How would it end?

Ortiz spoke loudly to quiet the crowd. "I call Stephen Russell."

Russell took the witness chair with some trepidation, but also with a determination to help Elena if he could.

"Are you Stephen Russell?" Ortiz asked.

"I am."

"Were you in attendance at the home and business of Simone the night she died?"

"I was."

"Why were you there?"

"I wanted to see Elena."

"Did you pay to be with her?"

"Well, yes, but—"

"Did you have relations of a sexual nature with her?"

"Certainly not."

"Then what did you do together?"

"Exactly what she said. I decided to help her get away. So we tied the sheets together and went out the window."

"Who went first?"

"I did."

"You left the room before she did?"

"Yes, but only moments before."

"So you were not in the room when Simone entered."

"No. I was outside. But Elena had already started out the window."

"But if you were outside, how can you know that the girl came out before Simone came in? It would be impossible for you to know for certain... would it not?"

"Look, Elena would never hurt anyone. There must have been... I mean if there was..."

"Impossible for you to know for certain, yes?"

"Yes, but—"

"No buts. You cannot know. Go back to your seat."

As he returned to his chair, Russell knew he hadn't helped at all. Maybe, he chided himself, this whole thing was his fault. If he had not tried to help Elena get away, Simone would probably still be alive. Who was he to think he could change the course of a young girl's life? What really made him intervene? He knew. Even if no one else did.

Once again Ortiz brought the crowd to order. This time he did it with an intricately carved gavel he carried with him for such occasions. He banged it twice before he spoke.

"Up to this point, we have heard from three individuals. I deem none of them reliable. The girl, Elena Esperaza, harbors romantic feelings for Stephen Russell. She may be giving false testimony to keep him from being held responsible for Simone Tejeda's death. The priest, Father Alonso, is unable or unwilling to confirm what Elena Esperaza may have said to him. His fealty to religious doctrine may be beneficial to his church, but it is not helpful to this inquest. The American, Stephen Russell, by his own admission, is unable to account for the girl's actions before she left the room where Simone Tejeda died. Therefore, I can give no official credence to any of the aforementioned testimony. And, in the absence of Comandante Delgado, I direct presiding Officer Garza to hold Stephen Russell and Elena Esperaza in confinement until such time as a decision can be made regarding their potential responsibility for the death of Simone Tejeda. If there is no further business before this inquest, I—"

"I have business," boomed a voice from a man now standing in the back of the room.

"And what is that business?" the magistrate asked.

"I have testimony."

"What kind of testimony?"

"Like the others. About Madam Simone's death."

"Come forward then. To the witness chair."

The big man lumbered slowly to the front of the room, then took his seat where the others had testified.

"State your name," Ortiz began.

"Mateo Chimara."

"And what is your relationship with the witnesses who have testified?"

"I have no relationship."

"Then what is your relationship with the deceased?"

"The what?"

"Simone Tejeda."

"She was my employer."

"What did you do for her?"

"Whatever she asked."

Subdued laughter rippled through the crowd until Ortiz's scowl put an end to it.

"Were you at her residence the night she died?"

"Yes."

"Did you see what happened to her?"

"No."

"Then why did you say you had testimony?"

"Because I do."

"But you just said you did not see what happened."

"I did not see."

"Then why do you want to give your testimony?"

"It is not *my* testimony."

"Then, pray tell," a flustered Ortiz responded, "whose testimony is it?"

"Simone Tejeda's."

The crowd's collective gasp was short but loud. Too loud for Ortiz. He banged his gavel again. It served its purpose.

"Say what you have to say," Ortiz ordered.

"As I said, I did not see what happened. But I heard noises. Yelling. So I ran up the stairs. The door to room seven was open. I went inside. The room was a mess. Everything from the bed was on the floor. Except for the sheets, which were hanging out the window. Then I saw Miss Simone. She was on the floor. Her head was bleeding. I got on the floor with her and put my arms under her so she could rest her head on my lap. I asked her what happened. That is when she told me."

The crowd couldn't believe he paused. Neither could the Magistrate. "Told you what? What did she say?"

"She said, 'I hit my head.' I asked, 'did they hurt you? Which one hurt you?' And she said, 'No, I tripped and fell and hit my head on the vanity.'"

Mateo stopped again. Ortiz filled the silence.

"What happened then?"

"She died."

"Just then?"

"Just then."

"Tell me again, when you asked which one hurt you, she said what?"

"She said, 'No. I tripped and fell and hit my head on the vanity.'"

"And that was the last thing she said to you?"

"The very last thing."

Flustered, Ortiz asked, "Why did you not tell someone before now?"

Mateo's answer made imminent sense to himself, "Because no one asked."

This time, the Magistrate quieted the giggling even quicker. Then he spoke with gavel in hand.

"This man has said he had no association with the other

witnesses." Looking toward Elena, Russell, and Father Alonso, Ortiz asked, "Is that true?"

All three nodded affirmatively.

"Then he has no reason to lie," the Magistrate continued. "Therefore, I am content to believe that we have heard the deceased's dying declaration. And as such, I officially pronounce the death of Simone Tejeda... accidental. Elena Esperaza and Stephen Russell need not be confined. This inquest is concluded."

His remarks were followed by one strike of the gavel, and just like that, it was over.

Chapter 41

The big purple and white house was searched thoroughly but no will could be found to indicate Simone's wishes for the dispensation of her assets after her death. Those who knew her best were not surprised by this, as they had frequently witnessed her protestations regarding the mere mention of her demise. She was convinced that thinking about and planning for death would hasten its arrival. That was thought to be why no legal documents were found in connection to her bank accounts either.

The women who worked for Simone, while exceptionally skilled at their current profession, were not fundamentally sound in financial matters. Mateo even less so. They had no real idea of what to do other than to find someone who might suggest a course of action. Because he was a longtime friend of Simone, a sometime customer, and obviously a smart man—else why would he still have his own sugar cane plantation, they reasoned—the group collectively agreed to approach Leland Bennett. They wanted to see if he'd be willing to help oversee either the equitable dissolution of their business or the continuation of it under a new management arrangement of what they described as *share and share alike*, or, *one for all and all for one*, which appeared to be the only clichés they could come up with to depict the only potential new business model on which they could all agree.

When the group approached Bennett with their idea, he gave it the requisite amount of thought and realized it would be an unmitigated disaster. He advised that the more appropriate cliché for the operation they were suggesting was *too many cooks spoil the broth*. He also realized that the last thing he needed, if his beach project were to succeed, was to be associated in any way with a house of ill repute. He did agree, however, to work behind the scenes with the appropriate bankers and lawyers to see that any and all remaining financial assets would be evenly divided between the girls and Mateo. He was confident this could be achieved as he was sure those same bankers and lawyers didn't want to be outed as longtime clients of Simone's. Yes, the girls and Mateo would each get a financial fresh start. And Retiro de Santos would put its once burgeoning brothel into its historic rearview mirror. A sad price to pay for progress Bennett thought, but in the end a necessary one.

*   *   *

While virtually everyone, except Russell of course, wondered why Comandante Delgado had simply vanished, no one was unduly disturbed that he was not around. The merchants no longer had to come up with protection payments. Bennett had already received and transferred the policeman's investment to the consortium. Officer Garza rather liked the idea of not being chastised constantly by his former boss and being seen by the citizenry as the tacit head of the department. He even gave some thought to hiring a deputy so he would have someone to berate.

But that would require more intellectual capital for planning and execution than he was prepared to expend.

Initially, the person who had been most concerned with Delgado's absence was Elena. She knew what he was capable of. Her concern was that he might be hiding somewhere, biding his time, waiting for just the right moment to silence her forever. To allay her fears, Russell convinced her that he had talked Delgado into leaving Retiro de Santos and never coming back. He told her the leverage he used was that in addition to himself, Elena and Father Alonso also knew that the Comandante could be considered a murderer. And if the policeman ever did anything to one, the others would immediately report everything they knew to the proper authorities. It was an explanation Elena readily accepted because she was so elated to simply have him gone. Father Alonso was a good deal more skeptical. He had known Delgado too long to believe he would simply leave of his own volition, but he didn't press Russell. He assumed that eventually, the American would feel the need to unburden his soul, and the padre was content to wait. Patience was a major building block of the priest's DNA.

Elena had been given a share from the dispersal of Simone's financial assets. It wasn't much compared to what the long-term staff acquired, but to Elena's father, along with the remuneration he had initially received from the Madam—which he had no intention of returning—the total was a princely sum. It was more than enough for him to feel that what he had done had helped the family financially. But even as he brought his daughter back into the fold and promised never to force her into such a role again, he could not bring himself to apologize. She knew she should have despised him for what he did, but somehow she found it within herself to forgive. He was still her father. He still worked every day to provide what he could for his family.

And Elena was convinced that in his own heart he must have thought less of himself as a man for needing to use his own daughter in such a way. She knew he'd never admit that, just as she knew she'd never ask him to do so.

Though he continued to wrestle with his decision, Russell eventually convinced himself that no good was to be gained by telling the world that the policeman was a killer. He could claim it. He could bring forth Elena to give her eyewitness account. But would anyone believe her? In most people's eyes, this girl was a runaway who had to be forcibly removed from Russell's home. Perhaps she's even a prostitute some would say, who had escaped out the window of a whorehouse. Why would anyone believe her story? And why, Russell asked himself, why make her go through all that? Sully her name just to give some measure of heroics to his? He still had questions. He still wondered what Delgado meant when he said *we* and *us* and talked about *our plans*. But the more he thought about it, the less he felt good about revealing what had happened.

Chapter 42

The telegram was precise. Alan Higgins, the Regional Assistant Human Resource Director for the World Conservation Organization would be in town for one day only. Russell was instructed to meet him at the hotel at one p.m. for lunch and what the message referred to as planning purposes. The American had dressed for the occasion. He wore a coat and tie instead of his usual polo shirt and cargo shorts. His sartorial decision proved to be the correct one, as Higgins was attired in a lightweight gray suit, starched white shirt, and red tie. The executive's deportment was as premeditated as his appearance. While he gave the outward impression of friendliness and interest in what Russell wanted to discuss, the American got the initial impression that Higgins was simply biding his time until he was ready to say what he had come to say. Small talk was covered before ordering. As they ate, Russell related the series of events that had occurred since he'd been there—leaving out the Delgado confrontation. Over coffee, Higgins was now ready to address the real reason for his visit.

"Well, Stephen, you've certainly had quite a go of it since you've been here. You probably never imagined you'd be involved with rumors of sexual misconduct, kidnapping allegations, even potential murder charges."

"You're right. I could never have imagined any of it."

"And neither could we. I mean if we had any inkling, any inkling at all… well, frankly we would have simply offered the job to another candidate."

"Obviously. But there was no way to predict all that—"

"You see much of what we do is dependent upon cooperation not just from international organizations, but literally from regional and even relatively local municipalities as well. It's vitally important that the reputation of the WCO be unimpeachable."

"Certainly, but—"

"And reputation is built and maintained not only at the highest levels of our organization but also on the ground, where any of our operations or team members interact with the public."

Team members, what a label, Russell thought to himself, as he began to feel that perhaps the hammer was about to come down.

"We're simply not able to accomplish our mission if the public feels there is anything less than professional about the WCO or its people."

"Mr. Higgins, I spent a long time explaining to you in detail how all of this came about. I can't believe you're blaming me for what's gone on."

"Stephen, we're not *blaming* you. We understand that things happen to all of us that are sometimes beyond our control. But just because these things happen, that doesn't mean we can or should abdicate our responsibility to right the ship when possible."

Russell internalized, *right the ship, Jesus, here it comes.*

"Therefore, I'm sure you can see why it's simply impossible for you to continue in your role with the WCO."

Russell paused before speaking. But only for a moment. "I can see why you might think so—" He was about to continue but Higgins cut him off.

"And we're more than happy to concede that your separation is absolutely not work-related. There'll be no mention in the official records of any performance inadequacies. It will simply be listed as a personal decision on your part to resign."

Russell couldn't help himself. "But what if I don't want to resign?"

"Then, well, I'm afraid you'll be missing out on quite a bit."

"Quite a bit of what?"

"Severance, for one thing. We're prepared to cover your salary for the rest of this year rather than simply compensating you for the actual number of weeks you've been an employee."

"I thought I was a team member?"

"Yes, of course. As we all are. But be that as it may, this is a very generous offer."

"And exactly why does the WCO want to be so generous?"

"Stephen, we're not cold-hearted automatons like so many for-profit corporations. You must have believed that or you wouldn't have joined us in the first place. Which… leads me to ask, why did you join us initially?"

"I had my reasons, Mr. Higgins. I choose not to share them right now."

"Completely understandable, Stephen. These separation scenarios are always trying. I've found that the sooner we can bring them to a conclusion, the better the individual generally feels."

Damn, Stephen thought, *in the course of a quick lunch I've gone from teammate, to employee, to individual.* "So, my alternatives are basically, what?"

"Alternatives? Well, as I see it, you have two. The first one is that you submit your resignation—which I've already taken the liberty of drawing up. It requires only your signature. And you follow that by signing a rudimentary non-disclosure agreement wherein the acceptance of our gracious severance package is yours... providing you do not reveal verbally or in writing the discussions we've had or anything that in any way could be construed as detrimental to the WCO. Should you do so, you will be liable for the return of the full amount of the severance as well as any other fees that might necessarily be incurred by us due to the litigation of your non-adherence to the NDA."

The pause was more than pregnant.

"You said I had two alternatives."

"The second is less than ideal. Official records will show that we have dismissed you for cause sighting moral as well as material breaches of your employment contract with us."

"Did I sign an employment contract?"

"Yes. Everyone does. And everyone forgets he or she did. We have a copy on file."

What started out a few minutes earlier as Russell's indignation, had somehow simply segued into regret. He couldn't keep from speaking honestly.

"You know, Mr. Higgins, I really do care about this sanctuary and the wildlife we try to help here. I'd like to hope it's going to continue to be okay."

"Rest assured, Stephen, that the WCO is already at work formulating a plan not only to provide for its holdings here but also to make sure that the community as well as the sanctuary will be taken into consideration."

"Will I, like Thackery before me, be responsible for training a replacement?"

"That hasn't been nailed down yet. But as soon as it is, I will let you know."

"And, when would I have to vacate… or leave my, I mean, the WCO's cabin?"

"Not for the next two or three weeks… assuming there are no further incidents. I'll get back to you on that as well."

Russell realized there was little or no point in arguing. The man brought a resignation letter with him. The lunch had simply been part of the process.

"I guess then, I have only one more question."

"And what would that be?"

"Where do I sign?"

Higgins bent over and pulled a sheet of paper from his briefcase. He put it in front of Russell along with a pen.

The American looked at the paper. It had the day's date, a declarative statement of resignation with no reference to any reasons why, and a place for Russell's signature. As he held the pen in his hand and continued to stare at the paper far longer than it would take for anyone to read it, Higgins said, "It's the right thing to do, Stephen. For you and us."

Russell signed.

*   *   *

Sitting on his veranda with a chilled glass of Puligny-Montrachet in his hand, Leland Bennett stared at the sea and felt a good deal of self-satisfaction. The stars were aligning. While he certainly hadn't wished it, the death of Simone meant one less investor to compensate once the beach project came to fruition. And the sudden disappearance of Delgado, while unknowable as to whether it was temporary or permanent, worked to Bennett's advantage as well. He had arranged things so that each participant's outlay included a fee for his oversight, as well as the transfer to him of their ownership percentage if for any reason they were not available or not content to continue in their participation during the initial takeover. And surely, that takeover couldn't be very far away. In his last conversation with the consortium hierarchy, he had been advised that lobbying efforts were going well and progress was definitely being made.

Progress, Bennett mused, *that's what's important. Looking forward rather than backward. One can't change what's past. No matter what you do currently, you can't transform what you did or didn't do before. The past is only there to haunt you, to silently chastise you for not being as good a son as you might have been, to belittle you for overseeing the decay rather than the growth of all that was left to you, to confront you for not changing as fast as the times changed around you.*

No. There was no point in dwelling on the past. Not when the future finally appeared to offer hope of renewal—renewal of stability, status, and perhaps most importantly, of self-respect. *Progress, that's what matters,* Bennett reminded himself. That's what he'd continue to think about as he looked at the sea's far horizon and sipped the golden liquid in the long-stemmed glass.

Chapter 43

The smaller the community, the faster news travels. A waiter, or a patron sitting close by, overhears a conversation. It's passed on to other employees, friends, or acquaintances. Information, private or otherwise, begins to spread like wildfire. Nuance and detail often drift away like rising embers, but even with gaping holes in context, some degree of content continues to expand. So it was with Russell's undoing. The story was passed in multiple fragments, such as the WCO doesn't believe him, there must have been some truth to the rumors about the American and the young girl, and maybe the results of the Inquest were flawed as well. Magistrates and the law are not always perfect. The outcome may have been wrongly decided. Perhaps the man, Russell, is a deviant. Maybe the girl, Elena, is a harlot.

Doors and windows, even when closed, couldn't keep out the gossip. Its effects became apparent from those who stared at the American, then quickly turned away when he caught them looking. Or from those who returned Elena's greetings, but whispered with others when her back was turned. Inez heard the natter and innuendo, but Russell had told her what did and didn't happen, and she believed him. So Inez simply blew it off. But one who didn't—one who saw it as the worst kind of prejudicial marginalization, plus virtual exclusion from the village's generally accepting society, was Father Alonso. At first disheartened, the more he heard the rumors, the more adamant he became about doing something about them. Additionally, there were other matters as well—long-simmering matters that were now exacerbated by these recent events.

Over the course of the last few months, but if he was honest with himself, really over the course of years, the priest had become disillusioned with the role he played. He continually wondered, even as he oversaw his parishioners, if he might serve his Creator and his fellow men in some different way. His inner turmoil finally came to a head two weeks after Russell met with Higgins, and played out in the priest's Sunday Mass.

The service had begun as usual and was conducted as it always had been, until Father Alonso reached the Liturgy of the Word. "The reading today is from John 8:32. Jesus, speaking to a group says, 'If you abide in my word, you are truly my disciples, and you will know the truth, and the truth will make you free.'"

The priest repeated part of the passage for effect. "...and you will know the truth, and the truth will make you free."

Now veering from the text, he began. "How many of us know the truth? The *real* truth. Not just a piece of the truth, a snippet, or some vague reflection of the truth that may come from a relative, friend, or neighbor... a second, third, or fourth-hand version of the truth that may, in fact, have no relation to the real thing at all. Then... how many of us pass on that infinitesimal portion of the truth to make it seem like we are in the know, we are the cognoscenti, the ones who lead the pack, rather than follow it? Well, you need look no further than to your right and left. That is correct. You yourself are often interpreters of what is true and what is not. You regale each other with things you have only heard. Yet you speak of it as gospel. It is not. It is a misguided attempt to make yourself appear to be important. How do I know this? Because I, too, have sometimes been a willing participant. I have tried to guide you to the light and the truth and the way... without speaking the *whole* truth... without knowing the *real* way. I have failed you, just as you have failed others. Today... that all stops. Today, we will face the truth together."

"There has been talk," the priest continued, "far too much talk about two members of our community. One, relatively new, Señor Stephen Russell. The other, with us all her life, Elena Esperaza. The talk about these individuals has not only been despicable, it has simply been wrong. Señor Russell committed none of the atrocities that have been linked to him. All of his actions were initiated to help Elena Esperaza out of friendship and regard for her as a person. Not out of some indecent interest. He has only tried to help her from others who wrongly sought to profit from her. And from one, who sought to silence her... perhaps forever."

A hush fell over the congregation. A quiet far more intense than that of the usual Sunday Mass. As the people sat in rapt attention, the priest continued.

"Elena Esperaza is a good soul. She sought only to maintain her chastity. And to tell the truth as she knew it to be. Her truth must be told. Bringing it into the light will make Elena safer than continuing to hide her truth in the darkness.

"None of us knows what has become of Comandante Delgado. But Elena knows what Comandante Delgado did... and if it is kept secret, he could find it in his dark heart to try and silence Elena forever. So... I will impart Elena's truth, and once everyone knows what he did, Elena will no longer be a danger to him, because he cannot harm everyone.

"The truth is, Comandante Delgado is responsible for the death of the Australian, Thackery. Elena saw this with her own eyes."

The congregation's collective inhale was audible. But it was not as loud as the one that would soon follow.

"I know this to be true," Father Alonso intoned, "because Elena confided it to me in the sanctity of confession."

The gasp was involuntary and universal—not simply for what the priest revealed, but for the fact he had just shattered one of the major covenants of the church—that nothing said in confession could be shared. Confidentiality in the confessional was inviolate. Until it wasn't.

"Yes, my children," Father Alonso said. "I know what I have done. I have transgressed, and I am prepared to accept responsibility from the church for my transgression. But I have done so in an attempt to make young Elena safer. And for that, I accept responsibility not from my church, but from my God."

Chapter 44

Russell had not been in attendance when Father Alonso shocked the faithful. The jolt was such, however, that it reverberated throughout Retiro de Santos even faster than the rumors that instigated it. Two days later, when the American heard what the priest had done, he was shaken. If he had told what actually happened to Delgado, Father Alonso would not have had to do what he did. Russell immediately went to the church to see the padre. Finding it empty, he went to the rectory. There, the housekeeper informed him that the priest had been summoned to an emergency meeting on the mainland with senior representatives from the Church, and that he would not be back for at least two days. Russell left, determined to see Father Alonso as soon as he returned.

Since his meeting with Higgins, Russell had spent much of his time contemplating what to do next. He still went to the beach each day in the morning and the evening. While he went about his typical cleanup and the search for any new eggs or hatchlings, he constantly scanned the rocks and the horizon to see if Minerva, or anything she might still have with her, had returned. Neither had. As Russell went about his work, however, his mind was full of questions without answers. Should he now reveal what happened to Delgado? But to whom? Officer Garza? Where would that lead? If anywhere. And still, he wondered, what had the Comandante been referring to when he used the terms we, us, our plans? While he didn't know, he wondered if perhaps there was a way to find out. Following his morning reconnoiter, he decided to touch base with the individual who seemed to know the most about everything that went on in Retiro de Santos.

"Stephen. Nice to see you. Please, come in," Bennett said.

"Hope I'm not intruding."

"Not at all. Have a seat. Can I get you anything? Juice, coffee, something stronger?"

"No. I'm fine."

"Well, I'm glad you came by. I've been wanting to see you ever since that nasty business with the inquest was successfully concluded. I'm sure you're pleased that's behind you."

"Yes. I am," Russell responded, "however, there's been a bit of a… well…. sort of an event since then."

"I heard," Bennett said. You know this place by now, Stephen. Everyone knows everything about everyone else almost as soon as it happens. The gossip mill is a bit like jungle drums in Retiro de Santos."

"That does seem to be the case."

"But you know, sometimes events that appear negative at first can turn out to be positive."

"I'm not sure losing one's job is very positive."

"It probably came as a blow to you, I'm sure. But large organizations, be they public or private or whatever, well, they're almost always overly concerned with their image. And if their name starts turning up in what they consider all the wrong places, then they tend to look for scapegoats, don't they?"

"I suppose so. But I can see where some of my actions didn't help matters any."

"My guess is, everything you did was in an effort to help that young girl. And that's laudable. You shouldn't second guess yourself on that."

"Yes, Leland, but it's not just me. I'm sure you've heard what Father Alonso did at church Sunday. He, too, was trying to help Elena and me. Now he's really in hot water."

"Father Alonso doesn't do anything without considering it in detail first. He did what he thought he should do *and* what he really wanted to do."

"But if he's forced to leave the priesthood, for something I was involved in…"

"That's the wrong way to think about it, Stephen. You're focusing on the past. And once something changes… well, it changes. Whether it's Father Alonso's allegiance to church doctrine, or whether it's that beach you were once tethered to."

"What? I'm not sure I know what you mean, Leland."

"Stephen, let me share something with you. Something that might help you think a little more about your future than your recent past. I can do that now because… well, because the die is virtually cast."

Bennett rose from the chair he had been sitting in and began to pace as he talked. "A moment ago, I mentioned change. Change, Stephen, is the one thing—other than death—that is inevitable. Life is change. And change is coming to Retiro de Santos, particularly as it relates to your beach. Very soon, an announcement will be made that eliminates the World Conservation Organization's stewardship of that stretch of beach that has come to be known as the sanctuary."

Russell was shocked. But he tried to keep his expression from making it obvious.

"Soon, the government will announce that the WCO will be relocating its conservatorship elsewhere."

Russell involuntarily interjected. "But you can't just relocate pristine nesting grounds. Sea turtles and other marine wildlife make their own decisions about where to go, and where to return decade after decade."

"That is a problem for the WCO... an organization of which you are no longer a part. There will also be an announcement that the aforementioned beach will be dedicated to private development under the authority of the Retiro de Santos Tourist Development Association."

"What or who is the Retiro de Santos Tourist Development Association?"

"That, in due course, will be me. And I'm sure we can find a position for a bright young man like you. You're college educated. You know the property inside and out. And you're already a part of the community. You would be an excellent addition to the team."

The pace of Bennett's words had outrun Russell's ability to initially comprehend them. He needed and wanted more clarity.

"Leland, what makes you think the government would go along with the kind of thing you're talking about?"

"I don't have to think, I only have to wait. You see, governments often do what's best for those who govern... and of course," he added sardonically, "for those who are governed as well."

"And this is best for both?"

"Yes."

"How so?"

"Let's just say that both receive substantial incentives."

"What kind of incentives?"

"Economic."

"What do the governed get?"

"Jobs. Work. Gainful employment."

"And those who govern?"

"Don't ask."

"Leland, I had no idea you were so well off that you could fund something of this nature."

"I'm not. In truth, I'm partnering with a business consortium from the mainland and I had to take in some local investors as well."

Snap. The references Delgado had made to Russell regarding 'we,' 'us,' and 'our' plans suddenly made sense to the American.

"These local investors," Russell began, "are you at liberty to divulge who they are?"

"At this point, they're silent partners. And at least for now, they should remain so."

Well, one, Russell thought, *will remain so forever.* Then his thoughts turned again to those who had been coming to the beach for centuries, and who might never be able to do so again.

"In this situation, Leland, is anyone speaking for Minerva and her brethren?"

"Minerva. Who is Minerva?"

"The displaced. Is anyone speaking for the soon-to-be exiled inhabitants?"

"I'm sure the WCO is making a case. I'm just as sure it will not be a successful one."

"Why is that?" Russell asked.

"Because economic clout," Bennett answered, "is more persuasive than altruistic clamor. That is one of the few things in life that does not change."

Chapter 45

The heat had not subsided. It just seemed to be getting muggier. Sweat ran down Inez's neck as she walked back to her flat from the market. Shank's mare was her mode of travel as she had loaned her scooter to Russell. He told her that he wanted to see Leland Bennett and she didn't think she'd need the two-wheeler. Then after he left, she decided that some exotic fruits and vegetables would go nicely with the fish she was planning to cook for the pair's dinner.

Russell had been coming to her place more often since his meeting with Higgins. There had been no specific discussion of what he planned to do next. He seemed content to let his time with the WCO play out, and she didn't feel like pressing him about it. A lot of potential decisions were just floating around in the air, both his and hers. But Inez assumed they could both address them when the time was right. It seemed, she would recall later, that perhaps those days were the proverbial calm before the storm.

*   *   *

While Bennett informed Russell of all the potential changes on the horizon for Retiro de Santos, tangible changes were already underway in the skies above the village and beneath the water that surrounded it. Their conversation held each other's attention to the point that they paid no mind to the bilious clouds forming overhead. The breeze started so slowly that it gave them no reason for concern. Even as the raindrops began to fall, neither showed any inclination to turn from their dialogue about governmental machinations and the persuasive power of one type of incentive versus another. It was only after their talk was completed—when Russell and Bennett decided to table their discussion for now and pick it up again sometime within the next few days—when a glance overhead brought about acknowledgment from Bennett that Russell might want to hasten his return before the skies turned from gray to black.

*   *   *

Long before Inez had decided on a trek to the store and Russell had resolved to seek Bennett's input, nature had reached its own conclusions about what should happen next. The intense heat of the last few days had warmed the water precipitously off the coast of Retiro de Santos. Warm air rose into the sky as the ocean's surface began to churn, increasing the size of waves as well as the power of winds overhead. Large air masses began to rotate and pull even more air into a cyclonic center. A trough began to extend the Inter-Tropical Convergence Zone as the northeast and southeast trade winds united. Some of the more superstitious would later say that the Mayan god, Huracán, blew his mighty breath across the oceans while Chaac, the ancient god of rain, spilled tears from the clouds to inundate any and all on sea and land. Whether brought by the will of gods or the vicissitudes of nature, the result was the same—the skies opened and the storm came.

*   *   *

It was all Inez could do to keep herself upright. She struggled mightily as the wind pushed her back two steps for every one she'd taken forward. Completely drenched and soaked to the skin, she continued to cling to the plastic bags full of produce that were getting closer and closer to ripping away. When the gale began to rip out vegetation, flinging weeds, plants, dust, and debris headlong, Inez tried turning and walking backward to avoid the onslaught. That slowed her pace even more, and her patience was the next thing to be blown away. *Dinner be damned*, she thought, as she tossed away the produce she had been carrying so she could use her arms and hands to shield her eyes from the stinging horizontal rain now pelting her face. *Just keep going... get home... it's not that far*, she told herself as she peeked between the fingers of her hands to make sure she was staying on the walking path and not drifting onto the road.

Her light, soaked, summer dress clung to her ample curves like a second skin, but she gave no thought to modesty. The only thing on her mind was reaching her front door. How she'd look when she got there was not on her radar. The next thing to go were her shoes. *To hell with them*, she thought, *they'd never be the same anyway. Maybe without them, I can even pick up the pace.* Which she did as best she could. Walking turned to jogging, which tried to become sprinting, but the wind was too strong for that. When she slowed down, she lengthened her stride as much as she could. *Every step gets me closer*, she told herself. Then she addressed the storm itself, "Give it all you got, bitch. You aren't going to hold me back!" A crack of thunder was the storm's reply.

*   *   *

By the time Russell turned from Bennett's winding drive onto the main road, what began as a cloudburst had become a maelstrom. Leaves and branches from trees were flying from one side of the road to the next. The American leaned low over the handlebars and tried to provide as little wind resistance as he could. Initially, he accelerated to a higher speed but the faster he went the more difficult it became to hold purchase as he rounded a curve, or had to swerve to avoid tree limbs in the road. He decided on a steadier pace as the wind gusts tested his ability to keep the scooter upright and moving forward. The last thing he wanted was to lose control and take a spill. Not only because it might injure him, scrapes and bruises he could get over, but if it damaged the Vespa and kept it from running, he'd be too far from the village to make it before nightfall. And the last thing he wanted was to spend the evening in the middle of a tropical cyclone.

As the gale raged and the rain pounded down, Russell kept his speed under control. He hadn't passed any other traffic on the road, but that simply made him think he was the only one stupid enough to be out in what was less like a storm and more like a hurricane. The scooter had no windshield so Russell was constantly having to close, open, and wipe his eyes while continually being battered by the liquid onslaught. *Keep driving*, he told himself. Regardless of the wet hell happening around him, *keep going.*

As he neared the outskirts of the village he could see that some thatched roofs had been ripped off buildings and shutters torn from widows. There was all manner of outdoor furniture, toys, signage, and debris being blown and tossed pell-mell across the streets. He quickly wondered how Inez's place was holding up. Surely she was inside, safe, warm, and out of harm's way. He willed himself to believe that. Then he turned a corner and her block came into view. *Jesus!* He thought. *Who is that crazy woman wandering down the street in this nightmare?*

*   *   *

They sat in front of the crackling fireplace, their wet clothes spread out on the floor to dry. Each was naked except for the covering wrapped around them, Russell in the blanket from the bed, Inez in a crocheted throw-rug normally draped across the corner of the couch. After boarding up the shutters against the rampaging wind, there had been some debate about who had the more difficult journey, but eventually, that gave way to getting the fire started, the wet clothes off, and the wine opened. The storm showed no signs of letting up. Winds whipped, and rain pounded. But at least Russell and Inez were both unharmed and in relatively good spirits. Though the coming conversation was about to bring the outside tumult inside.

"Think it's going to let up any time soon?" Russell asked.

"Hard to say," Inez responded.

"This sort of thing happen a lot here?"

"Not a lot. But now and then. Though this is ·the most ferocious for some time."

"I'm worried about the beach," Russell volunteered.

"What do you mean?"

"The way the beach is partially enclosed, a seiche could form. Depending on how long the storm lasts, it could eat away at either side of the natural barriers. If there's a lot of sediment deposit, erosion could happen quickly."

"Well, there's certainly nothing you can do about it now, not while it's blowing like this."

"I know. That's why I asked you how long you thought it might last. If it doesn't let up, things could get even worse. A storm surge… high-tide flooding… that could cause landslides along the hill. Mud, rocks, and vegetation could really play hell with nesting areas."

"But Stephen, think about it. This is just the natural order. I mean storms have been coming in and out of here forever. There's nothing anyone can do to stop nature. The beach and the creatures that occupy it have been more or less taking care of themselves for centuries. They'll do so again once the storm has passed."

"You can't go by what's always happened before," Russell began, "and with the way climate change is taking place, you can't even count on nature to make things right again. Plus now… it might not even get the chance to."

"What do you mean?" Inez asked.

"When I was at Bennett's earlier, before the storm began, he told me something I found hard to believe."

"What was that?"

"He told me that the beach wasn't going to be a protected sanctuary much longer. He said he was part of a business group that planned to take it over and develop it privately. You know, turn the whole stretch into condos and hotels for tourists and the wealthy."

Inez paused before she replied. She wasn't sure how to proceed. "But isn't that something that would have to be approved by the government?"

"He implied their approval was already underway. Nothing the right amount of money couldn't take care of where politicians are concerned," he said.

She tried another approach. "But you're not part of the

WCO anymore. It's not your responsibility, right?"

"Jeez," he said. "You must think I'm as amoral as he did. He even offered me a job when it gets taken over."

"Steven, I don't think you're amoral, I just—"

"And the thing that really gets me... is the fact that it isn't just a bunch of outside speculators putting up money. He said he even had local investors who helped him prime the pump. People right here in Retiro de Santos paving the way. I'm pretty sure that Delgado was one of them."

Inez felt like she was walking a tightrope, but she had to say something. "Did he tell you Delgado was involved?"

"No. But it makes sense, based on some of the things... I heard Delgado say once. Bennett didn't actually name names. He just said that when he got the last investor to come on board, the deal was pretty much sealed."

God, thought Inez. *There's no way to avoid this. He's going to find out at some point in time. And when he does, there'll be no way around the fact I didn't tell him when we were in the middle of it.* "Stephen... the truth is, I'm the last investor Leland was referring to."

Russell was looking at the fire when she spoke, and though it was only seconds, it felt like hours to Inez before he turned and stared at her.

"What? You're part of this?"

"Stephen, you have to understand. Leland approached me at the worst possible time for us. It was just after I found Elena in your bed. Then I saw you and Anne at the hotel. I thought you were a bastard. I thought you didn't care about me at all. And I thought... well, maybe I thought it was a way to get back at you. In hindsight, the money was probably more for revenge than investment. In my mind, I had been cast aside. I guess I wanted you to be cast aside, too."

"There's been a lot of time between then and now, Inez. A hell of a lot has gone by. When you learned the truth about Elena and Anne, why didn't you tell me then?"

"I don't know. I guess it's because I couldn't really do anything about it. Leland said that whatever the outcome, no money would be returned. And at that point, it was far from a sure thing. When you and I got back together, I didn't want anything to spoil it... especially if there was a chance the whole project would never come to pass anyway."

Russell emitted a faux laugh. "You must be a lot better off financially than I imagined."

"Stephen, when we first met, I told you my parents left me a sizable trust fund."

"Oh yes, you did, didn't you? In fact, during the time we've known each other, you've told me quite a few things, haven't you? Things I believed. Like I believed you actually cared about the work I was doing... caring for the wildlife... watching over their habitat... trying to make a difference."

"I did care about it, Stephen. And I still do."

"Yes, but not enough, right? I mean not enough to miss out on a profit... even if it means throwing the whole thing over."

"I've already told you the money was more to get back at you than to help Leland with his plan."

"Yeah, you told me that. But I don't think you would have... if I hadn't brought up what Bennett shared with me."

"Stephen, I hoped I'd *never* have to tell you. I hoped the WCO wouldn't force you out. I hoped the whole thing Leland was planning would fall through. I hoped we wouldn't be pulled apart again."

"And I'm just supposed to believe you, right?"

"Yes. You are. Like I believed you when you told me about Elena and Anne."

The gale outside was starting to subside, and the wind was going out of Russell, too. His initial surprise and indignation were being replaced with uncertainty and melancholy. He was feeling disillusioned, both at what she had done and the fact that she had hid it from him for so long. Yet he couldn't help but acknowledge, at least to himself, that he still clung to his own secrets. Secrets he was now even less prepared to share.

With no explanation for the abrupt change of subject, Russell said, "The storm appears to be slacking off."

Happy for even this momentary turn from emotional debate, Inez replied, "Maybe. Or it could be the eye. Which means more to come."

Russell jumped up and unashamedly discarded the blanket that had been wrapped around him. Then he started to get back into his half-dried clothes.

"What are you doing?" Inez asked.

"While there's a lull, I've got to get back to the cabin and the beach. To see what's happening."

She didn't want him to go, but she didn't want to wade back into the current gulf between them either. "Take the scooter. I'm not going anywhere with all this going on… and if we are in the eye, you'd never get to your place on foot before it starts up again."

"Okay. When I get there, I'll take it in the cabin, so it won't get damaged."

"Just make sure you're not the one that gets damaged."

Without really knowing why, Russell said, "It may be too late for that."

She couldn't immediately decide if a reply was warranted, let alone what it should be.

He softly closed the door behind him as he left.

Chapter 46

Days later, the devastation was still apparent. Many homes and commercial buildings had only partial roofs. Wooden planks had been nailed up to replace missing shutters. Electricity was sporadic. Some buildings and most low-lying streets had flooded. The water was only now receding, leaving mud and a multitude of refuse behind. The village and surrounding areas had all sustained damage in some form or another. But what Inez had said was true, the island had been through this sort of thing before, and more than likely would do so again. Rejuvenation was not unknown to Retiro de Santos.

The beach had its share of work to be done. Storm surge and high tide had washed away many of the sea turtles' nesting places. Partial landslides had brought some of the hill and its vegetation down near the water's edge. Cleanup would take earth-moving equipment as well as individuals on the business ends of rakes and shovels. Russell put in a request to WOC headquarters for what was needed. Even though his employment status was what it was, the home office assured him that help would be on the way.

Almost everything inside the cabin had been tossed like a salad when the winds took out the windows. However, the exterior, partially protected by the hillside, had survived relatively well. Russell found and retrieved deck chairs and a small end table that had been whisked off the porch and blown downhill. As he went about putting the place back into something approaching domesticity, the American was—if not assisted, then at least joined by the coatimundi, Bolivar—who accepted nature's knockabouts as part and parcel of ongoing planetary existence.

Russell had returned Inez's scooter the day after the storm and left it by her front door without seeking entrance. The two were working out their feelings of their last encounter differently. Inez felt, rightly or wrongly, the next move was Russell's. He avoided making one by telling himself he had too much work to do. It was a convenient rationalization. Though he had officially been dismissed by the WCO, the fact that he was receiving extended severance, plus his own ethics, drove his decision to keep working until his replacement was found. Also, with whatever free time was available, he was keen to see Father Alonso, whose pronouncements from the pulpit supporting him and Elena had become gossip fodder for miles around. The priest had returned from his command performance with the Church hierarchy and had much work to do himself, administering to the wounds his buildings had suffered at the hands of the cyclonic blunderbuss. But when Russell called, the padre immediately invited him over. There was much to discuss he told the American, which was indeed an understatement.

Russell knocked on the rectory door and had to wait only moments before it was opened by a man in blue jeans and a dark green T-shirt.

"Stephen. Glad you could make it. Come on inside."

The American was not used to seeing the priest without his clerical collar and robe. "Oh, thanks, Father. For just a moment

I didn't recognize you. Don't think I've ever seen you when you were… out of uniform, so to speak."

"Yes, I guess that's true. Definitely easier to tackle the mess around here in something more comfortable. Would you like a cup of coffee, just made some."

"If you're having one, sure," Russell replied.

"Come, let's have it in the kitchen."

As the two made their way through the small house, Father Alonso asked how the beach had survived the storm. Over coffee at the kitchen table, Russell filled him in on the work that had to be done and inquired into how the church and rectory had withstood things. The priest listed the repairs he was involved with and gave thanks that they were not as substantial as they might have been. By the time they were into their second cup, the social preliminaries had been handled and each was ready to address their particular reasons for wanting to get together.

"I just wanted to thank you, Father, for saying what you did in Mass about Elena and me. I appreciate it very much. I'm sure she does, too. It was a very courageous thing to do."

"I'm not sure how courageous it was, or certainly how wise, but every man eventually reaches a point where he feels he must say or do something if he's going to be the individual he wants to be."

"I guess that's true, Father, but by indicating what Elena had said in confession, well, you were taking an awfully big chance, right?"

"Actually, it wasn't a chance at all. It was very calculated."

"What do you mean?" Russell asked.

"Stephen, even though I've been in the priesthood for years, the truth is I've never been completely comfortable with myself or my work. I've always had to monitor… adjust… restrict myself in the ways I could provide help and guidance to others. Church doctrine had to take precedent. And sometimes… perhaps too many times… I felt that adhering to unbending dogma kept me from doing all I could."

Russell could tell the man he was having coffee with had more to say, so he refrained from interrupting.

"I knew that by disclosing something I had heard in confession, I'd be closing the door on my priesthood. Perhaps I was too cowardly to simply come right out and do it on my own. So I created a situation where the Church would have no choice but to relieve me."

"You mean…"

"That's right, Stephen, I'm not just wearing these clothes solely because there's work to be done. I'm wearing them because I'm no longer a priest."

"Ah, Father, wait… I mean…"

"It's just Alonso now. You can call me Alonso."

"Well… Alonso, I'm not sure what to say. I mean, if this is something that you really want, then I guess it's a good thing. Yes?"

"It is a good thing, Stephen. The right thing for me, and probably for the Church, too. They need to have priests who are more capable and more committed to working within their structure. I've finally come to grips with that."

Still a bit unsure how to reply, Russell simply said, "Well, I think you give yourself a lot less credit than you deserve. But I'm happy that you're content with your decision."

"Thanks, Stephen. I am. But that's not the only thing I wanted to talk to you about."

"No?"

"No. Something else is happening. Something I think you'll be quite pleased to hear about. Even though, I realize your situation with the WCO is sort of similar to mine now with the church."

"Yes. I'm just helping with the cleanup and going through the motions now. And I don't want to spoil whatever you have to say. But actually, things are happening that are definitely not good for the WCO, or the beach. Things you don't know about."

"You mean things like the attempt to turn the nesting sanctuary into a profit center for private business?"

Russell was taken aback. "You know about that? How?"

"Our former nemesis, Comandante Delgado. A few months ago he made the mistake of having a bit too much to drink at one of our church's community suppers. Away from *prying ears* as he called them, he divulged that soon he was to become a man of property. He went on to tell me where the property was and what was being done to obtain it. I think it made him feel very important to let someone know that he was part of these clandestine negotiations."

"And you being a priest, he felt his secret was safe?"

"Him being drunk, and me being a priest, he felt his secret was safe."

"And...?" Russell queried.

"I didn't think it was right. The sanctuary was just too important. And since he didn't convey this information to me in the confessional—which was still sacrosanct to me *then*—I discussed it with Bishop Alvarez. He was most sympathetic and believed in the beach as a haven for God's creatures as well. So we began to form a plan. Bishop Alvarez, having friends in very high places, shared our thinking with Cardinal DeLeón. And believe it or not, Cardinal DeLeón advanced the proposal all the way up to Pope Francis. Once he was on board, things started to happen quickly."

"What sort of things?" Russell asked.

"Things often achieved by the old carrot and stick approach. A little stick, but a lot of carrots."

"You mean the Church was actively trying to make sure the beach wouldn't be abandoned and made commercial?"

"That's right. The Church was working... I guess you can say at that time, behind the scenes... to see to it that the government would abandon entirely any efforts to transfer the WCO lease on the beach to private business."

"But," Russell interjected, "these business interests were spending a lot of money on lobbying government officials... both over and under the table."

"Think about it, Stephen," Alonso countered, "no business interests have more money than the Holy Roman Catholic Church."

"But why would the Church be so interested in saving a nature conservancy in some place most people have never heard of?"

"Though none in authority with the Church would ever say this publicly, it's not the saving of the conservancy that's most important. It's the *story value* of saving the conservancy. Think about it. For years the Catholic Church has been rocked with one high-profile scandal after another, like turning a blind eye to pedophile priests, condemning homosexual conduct, selling parish jobs to unqualified priests, and even spying on their own clergy via high-tech surveillance. Here was a chance to generate a totally positive story, one that could—and would with appropriate media relations from the Holy See—get worldwide distribution for making sure, even in a remote part of the world, that all of God's creatures are looked after. And that the natural world he created will stay protected for years to come."

Russell immediately understood. "It was too good an opportunity to pass up."

"Exactly," Alonso concurred. "It would generate the kind of positive public relations that not only benefit the Church, but the actual beneficiary as well, the conservancy. While the objective and the tactics might be questionable, the result will both appear and be noble. The sea turtles will be saved for years to come."

"When is all this going to come to light?" Russell asked.

"Very soon now. Some have probably been informed already."

"But I was with Leland Bennett just days ago, before the storm. Apparently, he was one of the major contributors to the private effort. At that time he thought everything was going his way."

"Then I'm afraid he's in for quite a surprise. Or perhaps by now, he knows already. News, under wraps or not, can travel like the wind in Retiro de Santos. And lately, the wind has been howling."

"Amazing," Russell volunteered. "Chalk one up for enlightened self-interest, I guess."

"Yes. And not just on the part of the Church. You see, the Church is making their support contingent upon local oversight. The beach must be staffed by local individuals who will be trained, supported, and funded by an operational agreement between the Catholic Church and the World Conservation Organization. And it will appear as if appropriate government officials were part of initial plans to make it all happen."

"So it will be more a part of Retiro de Santos than ever. And for perpetuity?"

"*Sí, señor,*" Alonso confirmed with a smile.

Russell immediately saw the irony. "And it will have all come about because of a Bishop with connections and a priest who isn't a priest anymore."

Alonso remarked, "I guess politics is not the only profession that makes for strange bedfellows."

Chapter 47

For the last couple of days, Leland Bennett hadn't bothered to close his doors. The breeze blew from one side of the house to the other, a poor substitute for air conditioning that had yet to be restored. However, it provided a depository for assorted bits of flora and fauna that slid across the marble floors when a gust of wind made its presence known. And the virtual open-air tunnel also proved an enticing lure for spider monkeys, squirrels, at least one redknee tarantula, plus a curious ocelot that strolled through the previous midnight. These uninvited guests didn't seem to bother the master of the house though, plied as he was with alcohol simultaneously medicinal and recreational. Medicine to dull both physical and emotional pain. Recreation to toast a plethora of challenges met, then lost.

Hair uncombed, face unshaven, dressed only in a white dinner jacket, polka dot boxer shorts, and sockless Gucci loafers, Bennett roamed silently from room to room stopping only long enough to consume whatever libation was at hand, or to make sure the cylinders were full in the revolver that was cradled in the inside breast pocket of his evening wear. Whether the weapon was to ward off unruly four-legged intruders or to simply cancel his subscription to existence hadn't been completely decided yet. There was much, he felt though, to recommend the latter.

The storm had flooded his cane fields and made even the most optimistic crop yield laughable. Of course, if he were being honest, which at this point he was, he had to admit that if it wasn't the apocalyptic weather, then it probably would have been the white grubs, wireworms, weevils, or other natural predators who had ruined his crops in the past and would have done so again given the opportunity. As most, everyone who had lived in Retiro de Santos for any length of time knew, Bennett was a remarkably bad farmer, overseer, and employer, whose head was only kept above water for so long due to the successes his forebears had achieved long before he inherited the keys to the kingdom. There was always the possibility, he reflected, of selling the cultivators, cutters, shavers, combine harvesters, and other equipment, as well perhaps, as the land itself. But he knew offers would be ludicrous after the amount of recent destruction that had been visited upon his once impressive plantation. Where does the landed gentry go, he wondered, when the land has forever gone to seed?

And of course, there was the ultimate blow. The incredible business opportunity that had literally been within his grasp had vanished. Like some malevolent magician's legerdemain, his vision of seaside skyscrapers, hotel complexes, restaurants, and more, churning out a never-ending yield of Euros and dollars, had gone up in a wisp of smoke—smoke mockingly not unlike that which rises from the censor in the celebration of Mass. Bennett even wondered for a moment if he could slightly detect the faint smell of incense. But no, it was only a daydream, an omnipresent nightmare now, from which there seemed no awakening.

As he sat in his study, stubbled chin in hand, he heard what he thought were footsteps. Not the footsteps of animals. Far too loud for that. More the footfalls of one not trying to hide his entry. The voice that followed was confirmation.

"Leland!" Russell shouted. "Leland? Are you here?"

"In the study," came the shouted reply.

Russell made his way there and spotted Bennett sitting not behind his desk, but rather in one of the two chairs fronting it. The American was both shocked and amused at the man's attire—or lack of it.

"Rough night?" Russell asked.

"Somewhat average of late. Have a seat, old boy."

Russell took the chair next to Bennett's. "I was wondering how you made out in the storm. Hell of a blow, wasn't it?"

"That it was, lad. And as you can see, I came through virtually unscathed."

"Well frankly, Leland... you look just a bit scathed."

"Come, now. Are you going to believe your eyes, or what I tell you?"

"A little of both, I guess."

"Ah, covering your bets. Smart fellow."

Bennett lapsed for just a moment, his head nodding. Then he quickly righted himself saying, "But see here, where are my manners? Care for a drink?"

"Are you going to have one?" Russell asked.

"Don't see why not."

"Okay. Then I'll have one, too."

"Sound decision, Stephen."

Bennett rose somewhat awkwardly from his chair and stepped to the side of his desk where a cart held a half-full decanter of brandy and four glasses. Bennett poured a couple of fingers into two of them, then instead of returning to the chair he had been sitting in, he flopped into the larger one behind the desk.

"So, what shall we drink to?"

"Ah…" Russell paused, then suggested "Survival?"

Bennett responded quickly. "Oh, no. Too dreadfully mundane. Let me suggest something much more appropriate. How about… failure. Let's drink to failure. Something we are both well acquainted with."

"Drinking to failure? Seems a bit depressing, doesn't it?"

"Depression, I have found, is highly underrated. Most people don't adequately appreciate the comfort found by simply wallowing in ennui."

"Tell you what," Russell began, hoping his levity would come across as black as Bennett's. "I'll see your ennui and raise you misery. How about drinking to misery?"

"Now there's something worthy, good sir. To misery."

The two clinked their glasses and each drank. Then Russell spoke first.

"I can't help but think you've had some bad news of late."

"That easy to read, am I?"

"Couldn't have anything to do with what we were discussing before I took off to beat the storm?"

"You're asking me a question you already know the answer to… yes?"

"Yes. I spoke with Father Alon—I mean Alonso, and he told me… by the way, were you aware he's no longer a priest?"

"Of course."

"But how did you—"

"Please, Stephen, even you should know by now the speed with which private information becomes public in Retiro de Santos."

"That's true. I certainly should know. But even though there's been no public announcement yet about the beach and all, well, I just wanted to see how the decision affects you personally?"

"I assume your own eyes are telling you that. But if further elucidation is needed, let me just say that the Catholic Church in all their benevolent largesse has fucked me royally. That project was my future, lad. With its demise and this losing hand that the storm has dealt... well, I'm basically belly-up."

"That's why you suggested drinking to failure."

"Indeed. It seemed most appropriate. In fact, let's have another."

Bennett stood up, retrieved the decanter, and poured another drink for both of them as he queried, "What shall we drink to this time?"

Russell, trying to get Bennett's mind off his somber situation, suggested, "Secrets. How about we drink to secrets?"

"Now there's a fertile subject, if ever there was one. Secrets, eh? All right, let's drink to secrets."

Both men raised their glasses and drank again. Then Bennett said, "You know, my friend, the thing about secrets is that they're terribly debilitating. All that hiding of information. Hoping not to slip up and say something one shouldn't. It wears one down."

Russell couldn't believe how much in agreement he was. He took another drink as Bennett continued.

"Tell you what, I'll start. I'll tell you a secret that I've been keeping, and perhaps in the telling, all the burden of playing everything so close to the vest—telling this person one thing and that person another—will be lifted from me."

"I'm ready to listen."

"Bottoms up first, however," Bennett said, draining his tumbler.

Russell did the same and Bennett then emptied the remaining contents of the decanter into his and the American's glass.

"The truth, dear Stephen, is that I wasn't the only one here in Retiro de Santos who rolled the dice on turning your beach into a money maker. I had some local backers you actually know quite well. They were... the unfortunate Simone, may she rest in peace, the still-missing Delgado, as if it matters, and brace yourself..."

Before he could finish, Russell said, "Inez."

"What? She told you? I would have thought you wouldn't have been too keen on her participation."

"I wasn't. I'm not. I mean, I guess I'm still processing how she could have done something like that when she knew how I felt, and when we were, well..."

"Know what you mean, sport. When you're sharing the sheets you often assume you're sharing a lot more than that. Sometimes you are. Sometimes you aren't. Oh well, that was my secret. Bit of a dud, wasn't it? Since you already knew. Let's drink to it anyway."

Bennett held out his glass, they clinked again, and drank again.

"Your turn," Bennett said. "Let's see if your secret tops mine."

Before speaking, Russell asked himself if he thought Bennett would have any reason for revealing what he was about to share. He couldn't think of one. So he said, "I know what happened to Delgado."

One of Bennett's eyebrows rose like an antenna. "You do? Well, my friend, as one Bassett Hound might say to another, I'm all ears?"

Russell then proceeded to recount his fateful night with the comandante. The chase, the struggle on the beach, the leatherback's intrusion into the melee, and the eventual disappearance of Delgado into the surf. When he stopped talking, Bennett had two quick questions.

"How long can this species stay under water?"

"Some, just under ninety minutes."

"And how far can they travel?"

"Many around 1,400 miles."

"The frequently menacing Comandante Delgado—"

Once again, Russell finished his sentence. "Won't be coming back."

"Game, set, match, Stephen. And don't worry. I have no one to tell and I'm not sure anyone really wants to know."

Russell simply nodded in response.

"Well, it looks like we each have about one swallow left, one more toast, then."

"Your brandy, your toast."

"Fine," Bennett responded, "let's raise our last glass to hopelessness."

"Jesus," Russell reacted, "are we going back there again? Look, Leland, I think it's a good thing that the beach will continue to be cared for as it's always been, and I'm sorry about what's happened to your plans but—"

"Please, no pity. That's not what I'm after. Just a bit of understanding will suffice."

"I do understand. But you may be taking this way too hard."

"Do you know what I have here, Stephen?" Bennett asked as he tapped the front left lapel of his dinner jacket.

"Where?"

"Here, in my breast pocket."

"No. I don't know what you have there?"

"Let me show you."

Bennett reached inside his coat and pulled out a Ruger .38 Special.

Russell sat back in his chair. "Whoa, Leland. What are you doing with that?"

Holding it in his hand, barrel pointed toward the ceiling, Bennett moved his wrist back and forth as he talked. "Haven't really decided yet. Been internally reviewing my options."

"Such as?"

"Well, fear not, there's no point in me using it on you, as you personally had nothing directly to do with my predicament."

"That's good to know."

"I did give some thought to introducing it to our recently ex-padre, both as a symbolic gesture toward the Church and because I'm betting he had something to do with the way things turned out."

Russell wasn't about to confirm Bennett's suspicion. He momentarily remained mum.

"And, of course, there's always the option of one to the old brain box," Bennett said as he placed the weapon beside his temple.

Russell leaned forward involuntarily. "Leland, no! Don't even think about that. Put the gun down, please."

"Not sure why society as a whole is so down on suicide," the man in his dinner jacket and boxer shorts said. "Everyone has to die sometime. What's wrong with choosing one's own time and place?"

"Well, this is not a good time or place," Russell responded rapidly. "It would make a terrible mess. As well as being a visual I have no desire to carry around with me for the rest of my life."

Bennett removed the barrel of the revolver from beside his head and let his arm drop lethargically. Still holding the gun, however, he said, "You must admit, though, it really wouldn't be much of a loss to the world. Worthy perhaps of only a few lines in a truncated obituary saying something like, 'Aging ne'er-do-well punches own ticket to Hades. Friends and associates wonder what took him so long.'"

"Look, Leland," Russell intoned. "Things can't be as bad as all that."

"Of course, they can."

Russell was afraid to stop talking. "Okay, so the deal's dead."

"As the legendary doornail."

"And the plantation's taken a hit."

"Out for the cock-sucking count."

"But... things could be worse."

"You think so?"

"Yes. Sure."

"All right. Tell me then. Tell me how things could possibly be worse."

"Believe me. Dead is worse. Dead is worse than anything. Not just for you. But especially for the people you leave behind."

"And just how do you know that?"

Russell didn't want to say. He had avoided talking about it for a very long time. But the more he stared at Bennett, and the gun he still held in his hand, the more he knew that he couldn't just let it go. He had to try.

"Leland, if I tell you... if I tell you how I know, will you promise to give me the gun?"

Bennett cocked his head to the side, raised the hand that held the pistol, and leaned the side of his face against it, giving the impression he was thinking very hard about his answer.

"If I believe you," Bennett said, "and if it makes sense to one in my semi-sober condition, then, yes. I'll give you the gun."

"Okay, Leland. Then I'll tell you how I know. And if you don't mind, don't interrupt. All right?"

"I'm on board, sport. Let 'er rip."

"Okay. Before I got here, about eighteen months before, something happened that made me question what I was doing, where I was or wasn't going, whether any of it—'it' being the way you see your life unfolding—was really worthwhile or not. Wait. Let me backtrack just a moment.

"For most of my life, I was an only child. No siblings. And that was pretty much the way I, and my parents, thought it would be. Then the strangest thing happened. When I was twenty-two years old, my mother got pregnant. My parents found it hard to believe. The doctors said it was definitely strange, but that it happened every now and then. Anyway, even though my mom was taking a chance on things, she and dad decided to bring the pregnancy to term. Lo and behold, nine months later I had a baby sister. My folks named her Eloise... Ellie for short. She was the most beautiful baby in the world. Of course, we thought so. But so did almost everyone who came in contact with her. I was away at college as she was turning from a baby, to a toddler, to the cutest kid you ever saw. And smart as a tack, my parents would say. They were hopelessly old school.

"Well, anyway... one-semester break I was home from school. And every time I came home, I'd make a point of taking Ellie to a movie, or the park, or wherever she might want to go. At their age, my parents were happy for the break, and at my age, well, it almost seemed that she was as much my own daughter as my sister. Anyway, during that break I mentioned, when I was home, my parents got the opportunity to go out of town for the weekend. The company my dad worked for was holding an event at some resort and spouses were invited. They really wanted to go, and with me at home, to keep an eye on Ellie, it seemed like a no-brainer.

"They left Friday morning with a plan to return Sunday evening. And that's eventually what they did. But they had no idea what they'd be coming home to. Saturday evening, I took Ellie to the movies. It was one of those Disney pictures. She loved it. I managed to stay awake through most of it. When we got home she was bouncing off the walls trying to sing some of the songs from the film and just going crazy like little kids do. I was bone tired from trying to keep up with her, and also get some reading in for a class that had actually given an assignment to be delivered when we returned from break.

"Well, the point is, I fell asleep on the couch... long after the time I should have already put Ellie to bed. She found a way to amuse herself though, by getting into mom's things in the kitchen. Particularly the drawer that had cake-making stuff in there. Like pans, stencils, cut-outs, and for whatever reason, one tiny little box of matches. The smoke woke me up before the flames did. I smelled and saw it drifting down the hallway from the direction of the kitchen. I was calling her name before my feet hit the floor. Screaming her name, I kept yelling and racing through the house looking for her. I found her cowering on the far side of the bed in my parents' room. By the time I got to her, there were flames all over. Curtains, drapes, tapestries were going up simultaneously. Scooping her up, I ran into the bathroom, pulled a towel off the rack, and ran it under the water in the shower. Then I threw it over Ellie and we took off. There was no way to go out the back door, it was already engulfed. So I took off toward the front of the house and we managed to get out just as the flames started licking the ceiling.

"There were already people in the yard. Neighbors. Some said they had called the fire department. I remember being able to hear sirens in the distance. Ellie was wet from the towel, black from the smoke, and gibbering away excitedly. She kept asking me if I picked up Louie and the guys on the way out. I told her no, there was just no time. But she wouldn't accept that. She kept saying that I had to go back and get Louie and the guys. I told her there was no way. Even saying they'd be all right when I knew they wouldn't. But she wasn't having any of it. She begged me to go back and get them.

"Just then the first fire truck arrived. I guess the neighbors told them who lived there, because as soon as one of the firemen got out of the truck and spoke to a couple of people, they pointed my way and he rushed over to me. He started to ask questions about whether anyone was still in the house, which rooms were located where, and stuff like that. At the same time, Ellie was beating on my arms and chest begging me to go back for Louie and the guys.

"I couldn't concentrate on what the fireman was asking me so I put Ellie down for an instant. An instant. Just to understand his questions. She didn't hesitate. She bolted as soon as her feet touched the ground. I hadn't even noticed she'd taken off until I heard screams coming from some of the neighbors. They were pointing toward the house where Ellie's tiny legs were flying across the yard. I took after her, and couldn't have gone more than two or three steps before she vanished into the smoke and flames.

"Then it happened. What was left of the house just collapsed in on itself. I made it halfway to the door and got tackled by one of the firemen. He and two others had to lay on me to keep me down. I was screaming, 'Ellie! Ellie!' But everyone knew there was no use. The entire house was flat now. None of the doors or walls or any of it was even as tall as a little four-year-old girl who had run into a raging inferno to save Louie, a spotted turtle, plus Mathew, Mark, and John, three yellow-bellied sliders."

"Also turtles, I take it?"

"Yes."

Bennett waited only a moment before sliding the revolver to the American's side of the desk.

Chapter 48

With funds provided by the WCO, restoration work at the beach had gone well. It would remain to be seen how long it would take for the sea turtles to return in numbers they had amassed in the past, but being creatures of eternal habit, return they would.

Russell was still waiting to hear about his replacement. There had been no word as to when someone might be selected, so he continued to make daily treks to the beach cleaning up any refuse that might have washed in with the tide or come down the hill, and keeping a watchful eye for any egg deposits from the night before.

As the American was walking back from the boulders at the end of the beach, he saw two people sitting just out of wave's reach on the sand. Maybe tourists, he thought initially, who don't know this particular beach is off limits. The closer he got to them, however, he soon realized they were far from uninformed sightseers.

"Alonso... Elena... what are you two doing here?"

"We were looking for you," Elena responded.

Alonso added, "When I saw you over by the rocks, I suggested that we wait for you here. Let you get your exercise in, you know. While we enjoyed the view."

"It is a gorgeous day, isn't it?"

"Beautiful," Alonso replied.

"And a special day, too," Elena added.

"Yes?" Russell asked. "What's so special about it?"

"It's our first day on the job," Elena quickly answered.

Alonso could tell by the look on Russell's face that he didn't understand.

"Our job here," Alonso said. "We're the new you."

"What? What are you talking about?"

Alonso answered. "We're the WCO employees who are going to be taking your place. Remember, I told you that part of the agreement between the Church, the government, and the WCO, was that locals must be involved in the management of the beach. I was able to convince all involved, with the Bishop's help of course, that I'd be the best replacement. The government and the WCO liked the fact that we knew each other. They felt that would make it easier for me to acquire the knowledge I needed from you. Especially after I introduced them to Elena. She impressed them with how much you had taught her. So much so that they were amenable to the idea I suggested of making me the manager and Elena my assistant."

"That's amazing," Russell said. "I can't believe they're going to pay both of you."

"Well," Alonso replied. "They are and they are not. The salary will be the same as they paid you. It will simply be split between Elena and me, sixty-five, thirty-five. In essence, they get two for the price of one. As an assistant, Elena won't have to come every day, but she'll be available to help on weekends and whenever it is needed."

"Yes," the girl jumped in. "I'll love working with the turtles, and with Father… I mean, Alonso. And my father is very pleased that I'll be making money that can help the family."

"That's great, Elena," Russell said. Then turning to Alonso, he mumbled, "Are you sure you can get by with that salary?"

"Stephen, you forget. I was a priest. I'm particularly skilled at living modestly. And frankly, after a year or two, Elena will be of age and more than prepared to take charge should I decide to do something else."

Russell looked his friend in the eye and said, "That's your real plan, isn't it? You arranged all this so she would have a real future to look forward to, right?"

"If things work out that way, then so it goes," Alonso replied, with a smile that confirmed the American's suspicion.

"And the Church was okay with this? I mean, you are sort of a fallen angel, right?"

"The Bishop thought it was an excellent idea," Alonso said. "He liked the fact that I'd be interacting more with four-legged creatures than two-legged creatures. He is a good man, Stephen, and even after what has transpired, he wishes me well."

"As do I. I'm very happy. For both of you. So, when do I start my tutoring."

"Why not today?" Elena asked.

"Why not?" Alonso added.

"Today it is, then," Russell replied. "Oh, I almost forgot… when do you want me out of the cabin?"

"Not until you're ready to go," Alonso replied. "If you agree, we can simply be roommates until your own plans are finalized."

"Don't forget Bolivar," Elena interjected.

"For now… roommates it is," Russell said to Alonso. "You, me, and Bolivar. Now, let's waste no more time," he said only half-jokingly. "How much do you know about olive ridley turtles?"

Chapter 49

Inez hadn't seen Russell since she let him know of her involvement with Bennett's failed endeavor. It didn't surprise her that he hadn't come over. It did surprise her that she hadn't gone to see him. She realized the degree to which he felt betrayed, both by her action and by her silence. But she thought perhaps it was best for both of them to give themselves their own space for a bit. Or at least that's how she rationalized it.

For his part, Russell wondered if he'd been too unbending. Certainly, it was a shock to hear that Inez, of all people, had been involved in a scheme to privatize the beach. A scheme that would not only put him out of work, but would also turn a sanctuary for marine life into a playground for big spenders. Anyone would be hurt and annoyed by that. Surely it made sense to take some time apart to figure out how he really felt. Or at least that's how he explained his inaction to himself.

Fate—be it random coincidence or part of some omnipotent deity's grand plan—offers a way of coming to grips with the unresolved. So it was that Russell's morning stroll, where he found himself by one of the few commercial establishments in the village that had more or less survived the recent storm intact. Jake's Java was the name of the coffee shop that locals thought of as their own. And this particular morning, Inez's scooter was parked out front. At first, Russell slowed, hesitated, then started to increase his pace again before stopping, sighing, and asking himself what the hell he was afraid of. Someone had to make the first move, he thought. Might as well be him.

Inez was alone at a table for two in the corner. He saw her but went straight to the counter and ordered a coffee. When the girl handed him his cup, he suddenly realized there was no problem being there in his T-shirt, gym shorts, and sneakers, but being there without a wallet or any way to pay *was* perhaps a problem. When he began to stutter, "I… uh, forgot my…"

Inez recognized his voice, looked up, and shouted to the girl, "I'll take care of it." Russell then walked over to her table with cup in hand and embarrassment in tow.

"Thanks," he said. "Mind if I sit down?"

"I would mind if you didn't," she replied.

As he took the empty chair at her table, he said, "I was out for a walk and saw your scooter. Totally forgot I didn't have a penny on me."

"Yes, my Vespa's been known to affect people that way."

"So," he began awkwardly, "how have you been?"

"A little ill," she replied.

"Really? What was it?"

"Oh, just a common case of contrition, you know. With kind of a side effect of loneliness. Don't worry, though. To my knowledge, it's not contagious."

"Might be wrong about that, you know. In fact, I've been having a few symptoms myself."

"Going around, I guess, huh?"

"That's what I hear." Oh, speaking of hearing, did you hear that Alonso and—"

"Elena? And the WCO? Of course, I did. This is Retiro de Santos, Stephen."

"Yeah. Why do I keep forgetting that?"

"I guess there are some places in the world where everyone doesn't know everyone else's business, but this certainly isn't one of them."

"That's for sure. Speaking of business, how's yours going? Painting lots of tourists's caricatures?"

"Needless to say those have fallen off quite a bit, with the storm and all."

"Oh, of course. I should have known that."

"But, that's given me more time to devote to my own work... oh... for Christ's sake, how long are we going to dance around this? I assume you no longer hate me, or you wouldn't be here. Or, are you just trying to be so very civilized about the whole thing?"

Russell stopped fiddling with his coffee cup that he had yet to drink from. "I don't hate you, Inez. I never hated you. I guess I was just hurt and disappointed... and at that time sick about what I thought was going to happen to the beach."

"I understand," she said. "Even though I don't want to admit it, I royally screwed up, and the last thing I wanted to do was to hurt you. That was never my intent. Oh, wait, actually it was my intent when I thought you were banging two other women when you were comfort-tumbling with me. But it wasn't my intent when I found out the truth. By then I was already in too deep to do anything about it... except, of course, tell you. I should have told you earlier. Much earlier. I realize that now."

"Odd, isn't it?" Stephen said, looking not at Inez, but out the window at a memory. "Sometimes the things we don't do cause the most harm?"

"Well, that was certainly what happened in our case. And

if I haven't already, I want to apologize for it. I'm sorry. I'm really sorry."

"I'm sorry, too, Inez. Occasionally, I act like a real dope. It's in my DNA, I guess."

She reached across the table and took his hand. He squeezed hers in return.

"But look," she began, "now that Alonso and Elena are going to be taking over from you, have you given any thought to what *you're* going to do?"

"I have given it some thought. Need to give it a little more. But I know what I'd like to do… and that's take you to dinner. Are you free tonight?"

"Of course. But we don't need to go out. I can fix something at my place."

"No. I want to take you out. I'll make a reservation at the hotel restaurant. We'll do it up right. I'll even wear a tie."

"Never argue with a man who wants to spend money on you. That I have learned. So, I'll doll myself up, too. Makeup. An actual dress. But no tie for me."

Her quip drew a chuckle from each that almost felt genuine.

That night at the hotel, there was a lone candle on the table. After Inez and Russell were seated, the waiter lit it. Its flame burned brightly throughout the aperitifs, the appetizers, the wine, and the main course. By the time both had passed on dessert in favor of a glass of port, the candle's flame, like their affair, was almost extinguished, and the visual symbolism wasn't lost on either of them.

"You've decided to leave, haven't you?"

"Yes," Russell answered.

"When will you be going?"

"In the next couple of days. Friday actually. That's when the boat comes."

"And what will you be doing?"

"Teaching, I hope. That was my original plan."

"You never really told me why you didn't go into teaching right out of school."

"I know. Kind of a secret I guess." Silence lingered for a moment before he added. "Some people say that secrets aren't always a bad thing to have."

"People say a lot of stupid things."

"Maybe you're more profound than you know. Then, of course, it probably doesn't matter. This is Retiro de Santos. I'm sure you'll hear all about it soon enough."

"Russell…"

"No. Please. Let me speak first. Then I won't be compelled to parry, thrust, or equivocate. Inez, it's been wonderful being with you. I knew from the moment we first spoke that I had never met anyone like you. And I don't think I ever will again. Not only are you beautiful, smart, and talented, you're also a wonder in bed. A veritable wonder. It's been one of the biggest thrills of my life being with you."

"But the thought of continuing what we have is not that thrilling, is it?"

"Too much has gone on for me to stay here," Russell said. "And I don't think you'd be very content at some land-locked prairie town in the American Midwest. The winters are a bitch."

"Well, that's one thing you've said that I can agree with. And it's certainly not the only thing." Inez reached across and put her hand on top of his. "Believe it or not, it's been thrilling for me, too, damn it."

Russell started to put his other hand on top of theirs, but she pulled hers away saying, "No. Let's just finish our port, and then we'll both be on our way. Me first. That way you won't be embarrassed by the mascara running down my cheek."

"Let me walk you home."

"Why make it even harder?"

Inez gathered her purse before downing what remained in her glass. She then stood, bent over, kissed Russell on the cheek, and walked away.

Chapter 50

Plans had been made for Russell's departure. Leland Bennett had offered to drive him to his embarkation point and the American accepted. Before that, Russell would share breakfast in the cabin with Alonso, Bolivar, and Elena, who would also come over to say goodbye.

The day came and Russell was up before dawn. He wanted to watch one last sunrise on the beach. Alonso made a point of letting him do it alone. Later, the three people and the coatimundi ate a hearty breakfast and shared memories of their time together. Russell shared one more thing. He had decided that he couldn't leave the two wondering if Comandante Delgado would someday return to plague them again, especially Elena. So he explained in detail exactly what happened to the corrupt policeman. No good person feels joy at the loss of someone's life. And these were good people. But relief was felt, even if unspoken. Then it was decided they'd say goodbye in the cabin, and Alonso and Elena would go down to the beach while Russell awaited Bennett's arrival. There were hugs and tears among the smiles, and everyone saying that they'd one day see each other again, though no one really believed that. Then Alonso and Elena headed down to the beach, and Russell went out to the front porch to await his ride from Bennett. As he sat in one of the chairs, valise by his side with Bolivar atop it, he thought of the first time he walked up the path and shared a beer with Thackery. It was a day not unlike this one, bright sun, blue sky, white clouds. That day was a beginning. What was this one?

Bennett arrived in his open-top, vintage Mercedes. Was it the last thing of real value he possessed? Russell wondered, though he promised himself he wouldn't ask. There was no need to use the horn to announce his arrival; the older man saw the American on the porch looking his way. He watched from the car as Russell put the coatimundi on his arm, then walked over and gingerly set him on the windowsill. Bolivar wrapped his tail around Russell's wrist one last time, then quickly unwrapped it and disappeared inside.

Initially, conversation was minimal as they traversed the winding road that would take them to the same cove where Russell arrived. Rounding a turn, the American pointed to a wide shoulder on the cliff and said, "We're a little ahead of time. Mind if we stop for a moment?"

"Not at all," Bennett answered, understanding that the view was indeed spectacular, particularly if seeing it for the last time.

Parked on the side of the road, engine off, both men sat and stared at the sea. Bennett pulled a cigarette case from the breast pocket of his coat, took out a single, and tapped it on the case before using his lighter. Smoke from the first puff drifted over the windshield.

"How can you leave a paradise such as this?" Bennett asked.

"No, just thinking how lucky I was to have spent some time here."

"Think luck has a lot to do with life, do you?"

"Not really sure. Maybe luck is just another form of fate. Or maybe we make our own luck. What do you think?"

"What do I think? Well, I'll tell you, Stephen. I think people go through life like boats go through water. They leave a wake. Some, like Father Alonso... sorry, make that simply Alonso, leave a wake of... I don't know, hope I guess. Yes. Alonso leaves a wake of hope. Others, take Delgado for example, leave a wake of angst or displeasure. Haven't heard from anyone who's at all disturbed that he isn't around anymore."

Russell couldn't help himself. "What about me?"

Bennett took a long drag from his cigarette and blew out the smoke slowly before answering. "You, my friend, leave a wake of misfortune. You don't mean to. That's just the way it is. Your little sister, your ex-mate Thackery, poor Simone, the aforementioned Delgado, I doubt that Inez is all smiles today, and of course, you know that my circumstances have declined precipitously since your arrival on our fair island."

Russell paused before replying, wishing momentarily that he hadn't asked. "Jesus, you must be glad to see me go."

"Not at all, dear boy. I've actually become rather taken with you. Just got caught up in your wake, that's all. Not your fault, really."

"Well, when I'm gone, I assume my wake will be, too. Then you, Inez, and anyone else that got caught in it will simply get over it. Yes?"

Bennett's reply was immediate. "One never really gets over anything, Stephen. One simply learns to get on with it."

The rest of the drive was made in silence. Russell asked to be let out at the same spot where he waited for the lorry that took him into Retiro de Santos. From there he would be able to see the vessel round the bend, then he could easily walk down to the shore and await the dingy that would take him to the ship.

Once there, farewells were exchanged. Russell's somewhat less warm than Bennett's. The American was still stinging a bit from the other's previous words. Yet as he watched him drive away, Russell asked himself if there wasn't at least some degree of truth in what Bennett had said.

While he waited, Russell sat on his valise and tried to make sense of things. Though he had never admitted it to anyone, he knew he had become a budding environmentalist and potential savior of sea turtles in a guilt-ridden attempt to somehow do penance for the role he played in his sister's death. Was it misguided? Probably. Did he fail completely? Perhaps not. Perhaps his involvement in Elena's life was atonement to some degree. He hoped so.

Other questions filled his thoughts beneath the white-hot sun. One raised by Bennett's comment. Was he really a jinx to those who came in contact with him, or were their actions what led to the outcomes? The answer probably lay somewhere within a bigger question. Is anyone the architect of his or her fate, or simply a captive of it?

As Russell pondered, he watched the ship arrive. Eventually, he saw the skiff lowered and begin its labored row toward shore. Rising, he began his walk down to the cove at Punta Olvidado Bay. Punta Olvidado. Forgotten point. The gateway for those entering or leaving Retiro de Santos. Saints Retreat.

Reaching the beach, he removed his shoes, put his socks inside them, tied the laces together, and threw them over his shoulder. Would his boatman be the same, he wondered? The fellow who warned him that boulders fronting the beach could rip hulls asunder if the sailor wasn't experienced, or at the least, cautious. And if so, had he really been talking about the cove, or life?

In the shallow water now, with the shifting sand beneath his feet, a young man with unanswerable questions was leaving. While on the other side of the island, an ageless leatherback turtle, immune to soul-searching, was simply coming home.

About the Author

Joe Kilgore has won awards for novels, novellas, screenplays, and short stories. His tales have appeared in magazines, creative journals, anthologies, and online literary publications. He is the author of *Insomniac: Short Stories for Long Nights*, as well as the Brig Ellis novels, *Fool's Errand*, *Dying Art*, and *Cast Them Dead*. *Carrion Moon*, the fourth in the series, is in the works. His other novels include *The Horse Killer*, *A Farmhouse in the Rain*, *The Blunder*, and *The Golden Dancer*.

Prior to writing fiction, he had a long and successful career creating, writing, and producing television and radio commercials, plus newspaper, magazine, and internet content for an international advertising agency. He also writes novel reviews professionally for national and international firms. He lives in Austin, Texas, with his wife, Claudia, an accomplished artist. You can read more about Joe and his writing at his website: https://joekilgore.com.